I0571707

INNER CITY YOUTH

INNER CITY YOUTH

The Comeback Show Murders

INNER CITY YOUTH

DJ Special Blend from Chicago

CTUIFIED
PUBLICATIONS

CITIFIED PUBLICATIONS

This novel is a work of fiction. Names, characters, places, and incidents are the product of the author's imagination or are used fictitiously. Any resemblance to actual events, locales, or persons, living or dead, is entirely coincidental.

Copyright ©2013 **DJ Special Blend from Chicago**

All Rights Reserved. No part of this book may be reproduced in any form or by any means without the prior written consent of the publisher.

Published in the United States of America by
Citified Publications Chicago, IL

Editor: LJ Wilson - wilsolj@yahoo.com
Cover layout: Hotbookcovers.com

10 9 8 7 6 5 4 3 2 1
Printed in the United States of America

*Dedicated to my mother: **Linda Fain***
I so bad want to be able to say, "Look Ma!"
I'm pleased you saw the first one

Chapter One:
It's Been Years

Inner City Youth?" The stage director stuck his head in the dressing room. His headset covered one ear as he scribbled away with a pencil on his clipboard. "Y'all are up next! Be ready in five."

My boy Kyle Lathon slapped me on the shoulder as I sat on a stool in front of a mirror. His voice rang strong with enthusiasm as he clapped his hands. "It's time, homie. Let's give these peeps a taste of all the hard work we put in over the last couple weeks."

Nerves shot down my chest. I took a deep breath as I tried to shake off the jitters. "This is it. I ain't been on a stage in twenty years, fam'."

"Don't worry, you still got it. And those people out there know us." Kyle's eyes lit up as the moment for us to take the stage presented itself. "Just feel the heat and let the rhythm hit you like it did back in the day. We got this. Ain't that right, Quiet Storm? You ready to rock the stage, dog?"

Gregory Hines, Jr. rounded out our trio. He resurrected his

stage name of Quiet Storm for the occasion. "About as ready as I'll ever be."

Our group produced an independent twelve-inch cut in the summer of 1993 called "Hip-Hop Villains." We got national airplay on radio mix shows, and we performed at clubs throughout the Midwest regularly. Our video got mad love on the call-in cable channel named The Box. It also got a few spins on BET's *Rap City* and *Yo! MTV Raps*. We came up on a little money that summer and split it between the three of us. However, "Hip-Hop Villains" proved to be our only hit, and we ended up going our separate ways.

"Ichabod Crane is indeed ready to do this." Kyle used his stage name to refer to himself in third person. His attention shifted toward me. "The ladies want to see those green eyes, Dr. Dre. You ready? Let's get 'em!"

It's true the producer from the West Coast Hip-Hop group N.W.A. used the stage name Dr. Dre. Plus, a VJ from MTV also put the name to use. Whatever the case, my peers placed the nickname on me growing up. A rare mix of green eyes with dark skin set me apart from those other two. My parents named me Andre Johnson.

Greg came to his feet from a black leather couch and shuffled to the middle of the floor. He stuck his hand out, palm up. "Let's say a quick prayer before we go on."

I smirked and strutted in his direction as Kyle followed suit. We placed our hands on top of his, and he topped off the pile.

Greg closed his eyes as he prayed, "Heavenly Father, watch over us as we take this stage . . ."

Quiet Storm wowed listeners with his lyrical skills in the early 90s. Most people agreed he wrote the coldest verse on "Hip-Hop Villains." After the group broke up, he finished his undergrad in religious studies, married a girl from his father's church, and had three kids. He served on the deacon board and stood ready to take over the congregation one day.

Kyle had a difficult time convincing him to do the show. But he managed to pull Greg out of the church, and he dragged me away from driving for the Chicago Transit Authority.

". . . in Jesus' name we pray, amen." Greg opened his eyes and gazed at us. "Okay, let's get out there and kick this show's butt. Inner City Youth on three!"

We bounced our hands up and down three times as they locked on top of one another. All together on three, we threw our hands toward the ground and echoed Greg's command. "Inner City Youth!"

My crew and I exited the dressing room one behind the other.

Cold air attacked me as we hit the hallway. I damn near saw my breath in front of my grill as I put on my hoody. "It's *freezing* in here."

The dressing room faced a hallway that led to doors facing the parking lot behind the building. The late January air whooshed in every time someone went in and out. About fifteen people graced the hallway right then, most with their winter coats on and unzipped down the front. We made our way through the hall and bumped into a thin, 6-foot 4-inch male with a round head. He carried a red and black baseball cap in his hand.

Kyle stepped up to be the first to greet the familiar face. "Goldie-Gold!"

"What's the word, fellas?" He leaned in to give Kyle some grip and a half-hug. He donned a red Eskimo coat on top of a black turtleneck and black jeans, set off by red Nikes. "Y'all ready to rock the show tonight?"

"We're about to put it down." Kyle snapped fingers with Goldie. "You can still go on stage with us, man. It's not too late."

Steve Hall went by his stage name, Goldie-Gold. He kicked a verse on three of our songs back in the day as a guest. Steve used his stage name in the streets, and most people knew him as a member of the Vice Lords street gang.

"Nah, man. I'm done with the stage for good." Steve glanced at us all as he gripped an unlit cigar with his forefinger. His voice rang deep like a bass singer in an a cappella group. "But my young protégé is getting up there tonight after you old men do your thing."

Nineteen-year-old Eric Taylor leaned against the wall near the back doors with a blunt hanging out his mouth. He went by the name MC ET. His red and black outfit displayed his ties with the Vice Lords. He exhaled smoke through his mouth and nose at the same time as he passed the 'B' to his hype man.

"Ya' boy does indeed have some skills." Kyle's eyes opened wide as he complimented the young Hip-Hop artist. "I heard you're close to getting him a deal with a major."

"I won't discuss my artist in detail, but I might think about managing y'all if you throw down this afternoon." Steve smirked. "This Old School to New School Jam is a good idea. Y'all be sure and represent for us old cats."

"We *most definitely* gone represent for the Old School." I balled up my fist and gave Goldie-Gold some dap. "We got this."

"Come check me out when y'all get the chance." Goldie-Gold gave Greg a pound. He faced us and skipped backward as he spoke. "I just bought a building off 51st and Ashland. Holla back."

We bigged up Goldie-Gold and crept toward the loud music and the roar of the crowd. The three of us marched by security through a door that led to an area near the stage.

"It's not as cold in this little space," I said as I removed the hood from my head and hopped up and down in place. "My adrenaline is starting to pump!"

Greg bent one knee at a time and kicked at the air as he shook his hands. Kyle rotated his neck as he stretched his shoulders from left to right. We checked out the act on stage. A female artist was singing like a canary. DJ Roscoe P. Coltrane held down the maestro behind her.

Noises sounded off backstage resembling glass breaking.

"What's going on out there?" Kyle's attention hit the hallway.

The bouncers at the stage entrance darted toward the noise. Screams sounded off along with a bunch of commotion. The three of us exchanged glances and trotted in the direction of the hall.

We got there and caught a small crowd gathered around a fight. MC ET squared off in front of another young man as his hype man held the dude up from behind. MC ET socked the other guy in the face with a right cross.

The dude's face snapped to the side. Blood exploded from his mouth and nose. It splattered against a nearby wall.

The hype man released the victim and old boy collapsed to one knee.

MC ET kicked the man in his stomach, hard.

Dude rose off the ground a few inches on impact. The young man landed on both knees, hunched over as he grabbed his stomach with his hands. Without hesitation, he threw up across the floor.

Screams rang out from the onlookers. Four bouncers in all black bum-rushed the scene and snatched up MC ET and his hype man.

"All is well!" MC ET bellowed the Vice Lord slogan as security dragged him away. "Got that ass whooped! Let's see your punk-ass tweet somethin' smart now, nigga!"

I recognized the guy on the ground as Stallion Pee. He had a major record deal and was scheduled to headline the show. His blue and black sweat suit advertised his affiliation with the Gangster Disciples street gang, the major rivals of the Vice Lords.

Stallion Pee coughed a few times. His face tightened in anger as he pointed at MC ET from his knees. "I'm gone kill you! Watch yo' back!"

"Fuck you!" MC ET used all his strength to try and crawl over the bouncers. "All is well, nigga!"

"Take that shit outside!" The biggest of the bouncers pointed to the rear entrance as other security dragged MC ET and the hype man away.

"Wait! Hold up! What's going on?" Goldie-Gold stormed in out of nowhere and approached the main bouncer. "What the hell happened?"

"He's gotta go, Goldie," the lead security explained. "They're taking him outside with the rest of the riff-raff. He's outta here. In fact, *everybody* out! Clear this area!"

"No, wait! My artist is performing on this stage, tonight!" Goldie followed the man to the back door. "You can't throw us out!"

Stallion Pee's boys stormed in from the opposite hallway. They raced to his side to see what happened.

Kyle tapped me on the shoulder. "They're calling for us!"

I whirled around and caught the stage manager trying to get our attention.

"Inner City Youth. You're on!" His arm waved like a windmill as it directed us to the stage. "Let's go!"

The three of us trotted through the door to the left side of the stage. The singer before us bowed and waved to the crowd. They cheered and applauded to show their love.

DJ Roscoe P. Coltrane held the mic close to his mouth as he bigged her up. "Give it up for Kee Kee Rose, ladies and gentlemen!"

She exited her set, stage left, as her smile lit up the spot. Her hand touched her lips and she blew kisses to the crowd. Each step she took inched us closer to going on. Commotion rang out from the hallway.

"I wonder what the trouble is all about in the back," Quiet Storm said. "I don't know what's goin' on with these kids today."

"Stay focused, Greg." Kyle's palms faced outward as he tried to keep Quiet Storm's mind on the performance. "We've been here before. Keep it professional. The crowd doesn't have a clue about what's going on back here."

DJ Roscoe P. Coltrane's voice caught our attention as he addressed the crowd. "Y'all ready for some Golden Era Hip-Hop!"

The crowd let out screams of approval.

Butterflies rumbled in my stomach a little, but it quickly changed into adrenaline.

"Put your hands together for Quiet Storm, Ichabod Crane, and Dr. Dre! Give it up for Chicago's very own, Inner City Youth!" DJ Roscoe P. Coltrane hit the button on the turntable and the instrumental version of "Hip-Hop Villains" thumped from the speakers.

The noise in the room escalated a notch as we sprung out and addressed the crowd. Greg sprinted to the opposite side of the stage as he pointed to the balcony. I skipped out and squatted down to slap high-five with people on the near side.

Kyle strutted to center stage as he pumped his fist in the air. His other hand held the mic close to his lips. "What's up, Chicago?"

The moment froze in time. A smile took over my face as I yelled into the mic over the Grover Washington sample to hype the crowd.

Kyle caught his cue and hit them with the first verse. "Callin' your name, but you fell into the game. You've been slain by the famed hand; you're screamin' in pain. You became the latest victim of a man who's insane. The mic is my weapon as I'm slaying perpetrators . . ."

Greg and I connected with the crowd and echoed the words of the verse in all the right places. The three of us glided around the stage to perfection. We could've done the show with our eyes closed and never tripped over one another.

". . . people ask me why do I kill 'em? I guess it's just a trait of a Hip-Hop villain." Kyle's verse ended.

One bar passed with the quickness, and I stomped to center stage to hit them with verse two.

All of a sudden, the music stopped and the needle scratched across the record. A thump came out the speakers, and then silence.

I reacted as a professional. *Don't stop the show. Keep going. The DJ will catch up to you.* I pointed to the back of the crowd and tossed my verse out there with no music. "Step-off, you gotta get-off, up at the let-off. Gimme some room, so I can wipe this sweat-off me . . ."

A handful of people let out screams.

They feelin' me! This put me in the groove. My delivery rolled out as if I were a young-buck trying to get his first record deal. The rhymes flowed out my mouth like a river, until Kyle got my attention.

"Dr. Dre!" he shouted without speaking into the mic.

Soon, I noticed Greg's voice calling, too. "Slow down, Dre! Look, man!"

I rotated and caught a glimpse of DJ Roscoe P. Coltrane's body sprawled motionless on top of the turntables. His skull and brains splattered across the stage and blood gushed from a wound on the side of his dome.

What the fuck? My heart thumped as I lowered the mic. "Oh, my God!"

Kyle fell to his knees. Greg rushed to DJ Roscoe's side.

POW! POW! POW!

Several gunshots rang out from backstage.

I dropped to one knee and ducked my head toward the floor. *What the hell is going on?*

Chapter Two:
Shots Fired

The crowd went berserk and scattered in every direction. A few people dropped to the floor with looks of terror across their faces. DJ Roscoe P. Coltrane bled profusely as his corpse covered the turntables and the mixer.

"Oh my God! Roscoe's dead!" Greg slapped his palms on his temples and took a step away from the body.

The stage director rushed in DJ Roscoe's direction.

Kyle put his mic to his mouth as he came to his feet. He tried to keep the crowd under control. "Everyone, please remain calm!"

I broke toward the commotion. People flew into my shadow as I bobbed and weaved against the grain. I rushed through the door that led to the hallway. Three bouncers tended to a body that rested on the ground up against a back door.

"Call 9-1-1 and get a bus out here now!" One bouncer shouted for help into his radio. "Get five-O out here right away. Shots fired!"

I came to a stop in front of MC ET's body. Blood gushed down his face from a bullet wound to his forehead. Organs oozed from a gaping hole in his chest. A puddle of blood collected on the concrete floor and soaked his clothes. Two security guards ducked to his side as one of them slapped on a latex glove and pressed two fingers against MC ET's neck.

The guard removed his hand from the body as he came to his feet. He got a load of his surroundings as he shook his head no. "He's dead."

What the fuck? MC ET's dead, too? What happened?

The one guard pulled his two-way from his mouth and addressed the others. "Did anybody see who did this?"

"I don't know." The guard with the glove on pointed at the door as he glanced down at the body. "There might be some people outside."

Two bouncers burst out the back door. The hawk came down on me with freezing vengeance as I followed them. I blew into my hands a couple times, and then grabbed my gloves from the front connecting pocket of my hoody. The three of us glanced around and noticed everyone scattering in opposite directions. People screamed into their cell phones. Cars screeched out of control as they drag raced out the parking lot.

One bouncer pointed to the corner. "Look at that guy chillin' with the backpack."

A young man in a Chicago Bears winter coat and a black skullcap lamped next to a bus stop. He rocked huge headphones that I'm sure partially served as earmuffs. He bobbed his head to his own music as he soaked up the scene.

We jogged in his direction.

"Did you see anything?" the bouncer with the radio asked. His breath appeared before our eyes on each exhale.

The young man pulled his headphones away from his ears and rested them around his shoulders. He made eye contact with me.

My mind searched my memory for a half second. I recognized him as someone who rode my bus route regularly.

"A dude ran outta there with a gun." He peeped over his shoulder at his surroundings. His head jerked and aimed between two buildings. "He went that way."

We took off and ducked into a corridor that stretched about fifty yards long. I trailed the security guards as we huffed at a steady pace. We got to the end of the passageway and gazed around at an alley. An abandoned Buick sat in front of a garage next to several garbage cans.

"Achoo!" I sneezed into my palms and sniffed twice to suck up snot.

The guard with the radio asked, "Which way did he go?"

POW! POW! POW!

Three gunshots rang out of nowhere.

"Oh!" The second guard's head snapped left as his body twisted one hundred eighty degrees. He collapsed to the ground.

"Smitty!" the other guard screamed as he ran toward his boy.

POW! POW! POW!

Three more shots came from our right. The bullets ricocheted off objects around us.

I ducked and dived behind a set of garbage cans. My chest hit the concrete as I slid three additional feet.

POW! POW!

Two more shots fired.

My heart thumped like a bass drum. *Who's doing all this shooting?* I lifted an eyebrow and rose slightly from my position to check on the other security guard.

Dude took cover behind the Buick. He snatched his gun out its holster and popped off the safety as his back leaned against the car. He frowned, gritted his teeth, and took a deep breath. Then he sprang to his knees and aimed over the car as his arms rested on the hood. Both his hands gripped the pistol.

POW! POW! POW!

The noise ripped a hole in my eardrums. I peeked around the garbage cans to get a glance at the other shooter.

Two more shots fired from the enemy's direction.

POW! POW!

I ducked for cover at the same damn time as the security guard. Footsteps scuffled into the night and trotted away. The bouncer came up shooting as he emptied his clip into the darkness. I rose to my feet and caught a human silhouette sprinting in the distance.

"Smitty!" The security guard fell to his knees in a puddle of blood as he grabbed his co-worker's head. "Oh, no!"

Damn it! I took off sprinting after the shooter.

His footsteps paced down the dark alley and faded to one side.

Still hot on his trail, I jetted down the pathway and ducked around the corner after him. Although I couldn't see him, his footsteps pounding the ground led me across the street and between two other buildings. I stayed on his trail as I paced myself through the corridor. Something slamming on metal became audible as I approached an alley. I stormed into another passageway and caught the shooter's shoes as he catapulted himself to the top of a garage.

I slowed down and side stepped beside the ten-car garage into the alley. His footsteps scattered across a roof that stretched fifty yards long from end to end. I kept pace beside him from the ground. His strides echoed across the roof. Then they stopped.

As I arrived at the corner of the building, I came to a halt.

Silence hit me from above.

I grabbed the top of a green, metal City of Chicago garbage can and vaulted myself to the top. My fingers snatched a good grip on the roof and my toes scaled up the brick. I rolled onto the flat rooftop and came to one knee. The suspect was nowhere to be found.

What the hell? I stood up and dusted off my pants.

Cold air whipped across my neck from behind. The garage was attached to an apartment building several stories high. The first set of windows went across horizontally about fifteen feet above me.

Where'd he go? Quietly, I advanced across the roof one foot in front of the other. I glanced over my shoulders with each pace, and then pulled the hoody over my head.

Footsteps scuffled around behind me.

My heart skipped a beat. *Oh shit!* I twisted around, raised my guard and bounced on my toes.

To my surprise, a squirrel shuffled around in one place. It scrambled and hopped until it leaped off the garage.

I exhaled a sigh of relief and grabbed my chest. *That squirrel scared the shit outta me.* I glanced around and tried to figure out for the life of me how the shooter got away. *Maybe he climbed to one of those windows?* I figured I'd head to check on that security guard and his boy as I moved to climb down.

A ball of flames sailed up from below out of nowhere. It floated high in the air and arched over the edge of the roof. The object traveled through the sky and began its decent before I realized the deal. *A Molotov cocktail! What the . . .?* It dropped right at me.

I pivoted and darted away. Three strides later, glass slammed onto the roof behind me.

CRASH!

Hot liquid splashed across my calves, ankles, and heels. A huge orange glare reflected off the roof.

I stumbled two more steps and crashed to the floor. A fire blazed only a few feet away. Heat seeped through my pants and shoes. *My legs are on fire!* I kicked around for a brief moment, and then rolled across the turf in an attempt to put out the flames.

It took about ten seconds to smother the flames on my pants. Smoke rose from my lower body as I glanced over my shoulder at the inferno. The fire blocked the way I planned to climb down. I came to one knee and moved to the other end of the garage.

Another fireball flew over the roof and descended in my direction.

You're kidding? I dived out the way just as the bottle shattered. *CRASH!*

I landed on my side and slammed against the adjacent apartment building. Flames engulfed the roof before me on either side. Both fires quickly spread to connect with one another.

Oh my God! I came to my feet as the heat bombarded me. A huge glare lit up the night. The fire trapped me next to the building and I had no way out. I examined the fire to my left and took two steps toward the ten-foot sea of flames.

The fire roared up another notch, as if someone sensed me walking in its direction and turned it up on purpose.

I scanned the area. *There's nowhere to go but up.* The bricks on the building gave a small area of space every several rows. *Just enough to fit my toes and fingertips.* I stuck my toe in the first opening, grabbed a brick above, and pulled myself upward. The heat on my back and the glare reflecting off the building reminded me of the danger at hand.

I scaled the building without losing focus of the first window above. Sweat rolled down my forehead. *Who am I supposed to be? The Amazing Spiderman?* Hotness grew more intense on my backside as I progressed up the wall. Miraculously, my hand reached a block of cement right beneath the window, and I managed to get a grip with four fingers. My foot went into the next opening. Every muscle tightened from head to toe as I pulled myself up another notch.

One foot slipped from a gap. The other slithered from its opening. I slammed against the building, but held a tight grip on the concrete beneath the window as I dangled over the fire.

Oh no! I huffed and puffed as I strained to pull my free arm up.

I kicked at the wall in search of a hole to brace myself. With all my might, I tried to hold on. But my fingers slid millimeter by millimeter along the concrete until I could no longer keep a grip.

I plummeted from the window to the fiery roof.

Chapter Three:
Hot

*W*HAM! My body slammed against the roof. "Ow!" I let out a loud shriek. Pain took over my entire body. I glanced up to discover myself surrounded by flames. *I'm 'bout to die!*

The stars in the night sky above twinkled peacefully, but the intense heat on my right roared like a lion. My upper body throbbed with pain and my legs stung from burns. I rolled over and came to one knee. The flames blazed at an alarming rate and trapped me against the wall.

I rose to my feet within an eight by eight foot area that got smaller as the fire spread. With no time to debate with myself, I pulled the string tight on my hoody and placed my hands into my sleeves. I took a deep breath and plowed through the flames with my eyes sealed shut as I stacked my forearms horizontally in front of my face for protection. Time froze as I leaped forward and landed on one foot. Cooler temperatures hit my upper body. My legs wobbled, and I tumbled forward onto the tar.

I opened my eyes and found my lower limbs on fire, again. "Aaaarrrrghhh!"

Instantly, I rolled around the blacktop and slapped at the flames until they went out. My heart crashed against my chest as I gazed up at a hot spot that got larger by the second. Enough room presented itself near the edge of the roof where I could brace myself and climb down. My lower body fell over the side of the garage, and I landed on top of a large metal garbage can.

A blue and white screeched onto the scene with its party lights on. The doors on both sides of the ride sprung open, and two of Chicago's Finest burst out the car with their guns pointed at me.

The bright spotlight from the driver side shined in my face as the passenger side cop yelled, "Freeze! Put your hands where I can see them!"

I stopped and extended my arms outward as I huffed and puffed to catch my breath.

"Don't move!" the cop on the driver side shouted. He grabbed the walkie-talkie on his shoulder and updated dispatch on the fire.

The other policeman bellowed out, "Turn around!"

I stood petrified on top of the garbage can staring into space.

"Hey!" He got even louder to grab my attention. "Keep your hands up and turn around!"

I snapped out of my daydream and rotated to obey the officer's command.

Footsteps scuffled around behind me. The officer made sure he spoke loud enough for me to hear. "Climb down from the garbage can without facing us! Don't look back!"

Fire truck sirens approached as I climbed down. The red engine rolled onto the spot as five-O put me in cuffs. They dragged me beside the blue and white car and slammed my chest over the hood. One of the cops frisked me from head to kneecaps. He stopped short of my scorched pants at the calves and ankles.

"What the hell were you doing on that roof?" Dude rolled me around to face him. "Did you fucking start that fire?"

"Naw, officer." I inhaled and exhaled to catch my breath. The stench of burning gas hit my nose. "I chased a shooter. He cornered me up there and started the fire. I was in a show around the corner tonight."

The officer questioned me, and I filled him in on my adventure. Three other cop cars pulled up meanwhile. The fire contained itself on the roof as it broiled away. One fire engine kept it under control.

The cop got a load of my story. He hit me with one question when I finished. "What were you gonna do if you caught him?"

I sensed sarcasm in his voice, but I played it off. "I don't know."

My hands remained cuffed behind me as they placed me in the backseat of one of the cars. Being handcuffed was neither here nor there to me. The root of my excitement came from the heat in the squad car. It baked in that ride, which was all right with me after busting out into the winter night with only a hoody and a pair of gloves. I soaked up the heat as firefighters sprayed water across the roof.

After the fire went out, they took the cuffs off me. More cops and detectives arrived on the scene and grilled me. I gave them as many details as I could remember. A female cop insisted I go see a doctor, but I declined. Eventually, we headed to the original crime scene.

We rode past the alley where the bouncer was killed. Two news crews camped out nearby. The Regal Theater evolved into a circus. Several news trucks extended their antennas in the sky. A crowd gathered around the perimeter of the yellow tape. Some people gripped their cell phones as they snapped photographs and videos. They escorted us through the crowd and into the building. A sheet covered MC ET's body as the crime scene investigators took pictures and questioned bystanders. The stage rounded off another focal point of the triple homicide.

Greg met up with me near the dressing room door. I caught

him up on the third shooting and the fire.

"What the heck just happened?" He wiped his fingertips across his forehead. "On stage one minute and all of a sudden we end up in the middle of a nightmare. There are three bodies!"

"I know, right? Look at this shit." I pointed at the open area where MC ET's body lay against the back door. Several shell casings lay scattered across the floor marked by yellow plastic cups flipped upside down.

Kyle strolled up and joined us. "Nobody's admitting to seeing the shooter. Anybody who definitely could've seen what happened has already bounced. Man, what happened to your pants? And did *you* see the dude?"

"Naw, man. I chased his ass, but he got away." I caught Kyle up on what went down in the alley.

"What were you gonna do if you caught him?" he asked.

This marked the second time someone asked me this, and the second time I detected sarcasm. I replied, "I don't know."

Several artists remained and were questioned by uniformed police and detectives. One of the bouncers bawled and sobbed about his coworker's death as a few people tried to console him.

"We shouldn't even be here." Greg frowned as he glanced across the room. His eyes closed and his hands came together. One hand palmed the other. "Forgive me, Father God for forsaking you."

"Wait a minute. This ain't our fault, man." Kyle jumped in and addressed Greg. "You ain't forsake anybody, dude. Don't start with that."

"I knew this was a bad idea," Greg responded as wrinkles formed between his eyebrows. "I rearranged my entire life to rehearse for this so you can live out your pipe dreams. Look where it's gotten us? This group was a bad idea twenty years ago, and it's a bad idea now."

"I'm sick of hearing your mouth!" Kyle stormed in Greg's

direction. "If you don't want to do this, then stop comin' around!"

Greg dropped his fists to his sides and poked out his chest. Kyle stopped inches in front of him as they stared each other down.

"Hey, y'all chill with that!" I stepped between them and shoved them apart. "This ain't the time or the place for this. Three people died tonight."

"Right, and I'm not trying to be a part of this scene anymore. Understand?" Greg stuck out his chin and threw his open palms up. He twirled around with an attitude and strutted away.

"Gone then!" Kyle shouted in his direction as he reached over me.

Realizing we caused a scene, I shoved Kyle in the opposite direction. "Slow down, dog. Let 'im walk away."

"I'm sick and tired of hearing his mouth." Kyle stopped trying to climb over me as he allowed me to push him around the corner. "He's always been a big holier-than-thou built nigga."

"I feel you, man. Just chill. We can talk about that later." I released him as he stopped resisting. "This is a bit much for us all to absorb."

The singer that took the stage before us sat sobbing in the corner. Two detectives stood over her as they asked her questions. The male detective wore a wrinkled gray suit and a brown tie under a trench coat. His partner's coat remained tied in front, but that didn't hide her athletic build. Lines in her neck showed she worked out regularly. The man wrote down notes with a pen and pad, and the lady punched away on a digital tablet. They finished with the singer and approached Kyle and me for questioning.

"I'm Detective Timms." The man introduced himself as he stood before us at 5-foot-10. He reminded me of Nick Nolte with a thick mustache. "This is my partner, McMahon. We understand you guys were on the stage when this happened. What do you know?"

". . . and we looked up and DJ Roscoe's brains were blown across his turntables." Kyle gave his recollection of what happened. "Greg and I tried to keep the crowd calm as the stage manager gave Roscoe mouth to mouth. It was a lost cause, though."

McMahon jumped in and asked me a question in a cool and collected voice. "And *you're* the one that chased the shooter down the alley, right?"

"Yeah, but I didn't get a good look at him." I filled the detectives in on exactly what happened, almost.

"So the perpetrator started the fire by tossing two Molotov cocktails onto the roof of the garage?" Detective Timms rubbed the stubble on his chin. "Interesting."

I checked him out closely as he scribbled on his notepad.

Timms eyeballed me before he asked his next question with his scratchy voice. "What were you gonna do if you caught him?"

I got mad. The third time was a charm, and I knew it wouldn't be the last. "Look, I'm the president of the Neighborhood Watch and I gave chase by reflex 'cause I wanted to help. I don't know what I would've done if I caught him!"

Detectives Timms and McMahon made eye contact with each other.

"We may need to ask you guys more questions in the future, so don't leave town. Also, you should get those burns checked out." Timms eyeballed my ankles as he handed us both a business card. "If you think of anything else, give us a call. Three of you took the stage with the DJ, right? Where's the other guy?"

We pointed them across the room to Greg as he spoke to other detectives. They headed his way as Kyle pulled out his cell phone. He owned a 'smartphone.' A huge, fancy screen rested in the palm of his hands. My regular old flip phone failed in comparison. I only used it to talk, as I knew nothing about new technology. Kyle shined when it came to computers and electronic equipment. From my understanding, or lack thereof, he got us a spot in the concert through the Internet.

"What the hell?" Kyle got excited. "Wow! This nigga is stupid!"

My curiosity hit level ten. "What?"

"Stallion Pee's tweeting about the murder! I can't believe this!" Kyle swiped his finger across the screen.

"You know I don't know nothin' about no tweetin'." I grew more frustrated. "What you talking about?"

Kyle flipped his screen around so I could catch a glimpse. A picture of Stallion Pee with his trademark dreadlocks hanging in his face appeared next to a short paragraph. It read: *MC ET wanted to be just like us #LMAO! That nigga is #dead now. Ha!*

"What does LMAO mean?" I asked as I got even more confused.

"Laughing my ass off." Kyle swiped his finger across the screen and flipped it around again so I could see. The same picture of Stallion Pee showed next to another sentence: *All Is Well niggaz is dry snitching #Shhhhhh.*

I frowned and raised one eyebrow. "Is that the stuff Stallion Pee is saying?"

"Yeah. His dumb-ass is sending this out for the world to see." Kyle twisted his lips to the side. "Can't believe he's basically laughing at MC ET's death and making a mockery of the situation. The second message is suggesting the Vice Lords are making the police believe he did it."

"Maybe he did do it," I added. "MC ET and Stallion Pee got into it right before we went on stage, right?"

"Yeah, but these messages are a bad move whether he did it or not." Kyle turned off the screen and stuck the phone in his pocket. "Forget about him. This may be jacked up, but I'm about to go outside and get in front of those cameras. I know those news trucks are looking for witnesses."

I shouldn't have been surprised, but I was. "What!"

"We gotta take the chance to be seen while the chance is there." He zipped up his coat and motioned toward the doors. "You comin'?"

I knew Kyle since the first day of our freshman year at Whitney Young High School. We had a ball and created a lot of memories, but I couldn't be down anymore. Exploiting those cameras was in bad taste to me. "Look man, I think Greg was right. I'm quitting the group, too."

"What?" Kyle showed a look of confusion. "Y'all trippin', man. We've put in so much work, and we have another show comin' up."

"This just ain't me anymore, but it's you all the way." I tried to sugarcoat the situation the best I could. "Go on ahead and get out there, dog. I'm fallin' back."

Kyle twisted his lips and shook his head. He let out a sigh as he pulled his skullcap over his ears and headed outside.

I cooperated with the investigators and answered questions for another forty-five minutes or so. Then it happened.

A heavy-set, light-skinned woman burst into the back hallway. Two officers flanked her as they tried to calm her down. Tears rushed down her face, and she sobbed heavily as she sprinted toward the body against the door. She ripped the sheet from over MC ET's head, dropped to her knees, and bawled out of control. Crime scene investigators tried to calm her down as she screamed to God asking, "Why take my son!"

My mind briefly went into shock. I recognized the woman from college. Antoinette Miller went to Northern Illinois University with me. I hadn't seen her in years, and this was an unfortunate way for us to cross paths. I kept my distance as a female officer consoled her and led her away from the body. *That's Antoinette Miller's son? Wow, what a small world!*

Five minutes later, I decided I couldn't take the crime scene anymore. I searched for a discreet exit and observed police questioning a janitor in his sixties. His dark skin and green eyes embedded in my head. I strolled past without thinking much of it. Eventually, I stopped in my tracks. *He looks familiar.*

I doubled back to address the man speaking to the cops. The police remained in the same spot, but the janitor vanished. I combed the place for a couple minutes but found no trace of him. *I must be trippin'.*

Cold air hit the skin around my ankles and my calves stung as I ducked out the building through a side door. Burn marks and holes showed along the bottom of my jeans and on my shoes. I zipped up my coat and tossed on my hood as I stepped into the winter night. The crowd remained around the yellow tape outside the building. Bystanders snapped pictures and videos of me as I marched on. As I climbed into the Chevy Blazer, the crowd convicted Stallion Pee of the murders.

"He *did* do it! He said it on his Twitter page," one girl yelled.

A few seconds later, a male voice came from the opposite direction. "Stallion Pee blew away MC ET, DJ Roscoe, and one of the security guards. That nigga is crazy!"

Before I closed the car door, someone else's voice traveled through the air. "The Vice Lords are gonna get Stallion Pee's ass!"

My instinct kicked in. *This is far from over.*

Chapter Four:
Home Sweet Home

At home I caught Colisa when she first peeped at my burns, yet didn't glance my way for another fifteen minutes. She gave me the silent treatment. Her lips twisted, and her eyes rolled as she pranced around the bedroom. She switched those thick, voluptuous, caramel skinned curves into the bathroom and almost slammed the door.

Colisa finally got a good glimpse at my calf when she came out.

"Lord, look at your leg!" Her eyes shot open, and she placed her palm on her chest. "You okay? This is no time to be avoiding the doctor."

"Oh, you're talkin' to me now?" I sat on the edge of the bed and rested a foot flat on the mattress. "I'm okay. This one scar is just a little bigger than the others. It stings like hell, but I'll be all right. It looks worse than it feels."

"It's all red and swollen." She sat beside me, snatched the wet rag out of my hand, and blotted the skin surrounding my wound. "You're driving me crazy with all your recent stunts."

"Three people got shot." I positioned myself as she attempted to comfort me. "I reacted by reflex . . . just wanted to help."

"There's nothing wrong with wanting to help people." She sat upright and put her hands on her hips. "Think about this, though. What if you would've gotten seriously hurt?"

"But I didn't." My eyebrows tightened as I stared in her eyes. "Don't start with that tonight. Enough happened already. Okay?"

Colisa frowned as she inhaled and exhaled deeply. Her nostrils flared, and I could tell she wanted to snap back at me. But her eyes softened as she looked me up and down. Her lips twisted to the left. "You're supposed to go back to work Monday. How you gone drive a bus like that?"

Although Colisa majored in finance and I majored in criminal justice, we both worked for the Chicago Transit Authority. Our undergrad degrees hung over the fireplace in the living room, slightly mocking us.

"I should be okay." I took two weeks off to rehearse for the show and the vacation had ended. "This ain't gone stop me from going in. I'm good."

She frowned a little and turned her head in the other direction. The silence rang out so loud between us that one could hear a pin drop four blocks away.

I sensed an attitude ever since I got in from the night's events. "What's on your mind?"

Colisa exhaled and held her fingertips to her forehead as she nodded back and forward. "I'm tired, Andre."

Okay, here we go. She's about to start trippin'. I braced myself.

"I prepared breakfast this morning, served it, and cleaned up." She came to her feet and shifted her weight to one leg. "I spent the day driving the Number Twenty up and down Madison Avenue. An old lady spilled a cup of coffee on me. Fifteen minutes later, a bum rubbed up against the soggy stain and smashed his pissy smell into my coat."

Okay, she had a bad day. My wife unloaded her frustrations on me.

"I stopped at the bank, then fought traffic all the way to pick up the baby." She paced along the foot of the bed. "I get home to find the place a mess, and your knuckle-headed nephew sitting around with his friends smoking weed and playing video games!"

Those words came directly from my high school sweetheart, the woman I'd asked to marry right after college. Colisa Garrett-Johnson hyphenated her last name and agreed to spend the rest of her life with me. We saw eye to eye about a lot of things and combined our resources at a young age. As a couple, we did a good job of being responsible and stacking cheese along the years. Only ten and a half more years stood between us owning our home.

My nephew stayed with us off and on. Colisa killed herself to keep our place spotless. Definitely one benefit of being with her. She ranked as the cleanest person ever. However, the added load my nephew brought when he stayed with us frustrated her sometimes.

"When you gone talk to him about pulling his own weight around here?" She posed directly in front of me with her fist on her waist. "I asked you time and time again to speak to him about smoking in the house. When you gone do something?"

I got offended because her tone insinuated that her having a bad day was my fault. So I gave her as much sarcasm as humanly possible. "Soon."

"Soon?" Her face balled up even more as her eyes lowered. "Soon? You need to stop saying that and make it happen. You act like he can do no wrong!"

"Look, you're trippin' me out right now." I rocked a frown of my own as I put bass in my voice. My feet swung around to the floor and I stood. "I ain't tryna hear this. You need to take that racket to the back of the bus."

"Don't talk to me like I'm some sort of teenager making too much noise on the Number Nine." Colisa stormed in front of me and stuck her finger in my face. "Why won't you take this seriously and say something to him right now?"

I slapped her hand out the way and yelled to the top of my voice. "Because I'm tired! In case you forgot, I just got shot at!"

"What's the matter, daddy?" The sweetest voice in the world came out of nowhere. Our daughter Linda stood in the doorway rubbing her eyes and holding a purple stuffed animal. Pink balls and barrettes hung from her pigtails.

My heart dropped when I laid eyes on her. *No she didn't just see her daddy being mean to her mother.* I dug deep inside and reached for the most sincere 'daddy's little girl' voice I could find. "Hey pumpkin. Daddy's okay. Mommy is doing just fine, too. What you doin' outta bed, baby girl?"

"I heard you and Mommy yelling." Our daughter's eyebrows went up in the most innocent way. "You guys woke me up."

"I'm sorry, baby." Colisa plastered on a huge smile and rushed to scoop her up.

"Why are you fighting?" Linda stuck out her arms to be picked up. "Are you and daddy getting a divorce?"

I chuckled. We argued over different things when we got stressed out, just like any couple. However, breaking up was the last thing that could ever happen to our marriage.

"Oh no, sweetie." My wife comforted the four year old in her arms. "Mommy and Daddy are just tired. Come on; let's put you back to bed."

"Dorian's room smells funny again," the baby said as she held on tight to her mother.

"That's his funny smelling cologne," Colisa lied. She toted Linda away toward her room as she made eye contact with me. "Don't worry. Your daddy is going to talk to Dorian about his funny smelling cologne, *tonight.*"

Our eyes remained connected as she carried Linda out the room. I twisted my mouth and exhaled deeply as the pain kicked up a notch. The rag rested on the foot of the bed. I grabbed it and bounced into the bathroom before dampening it some more with cold water. The towel gave little relief as I tried to figure out what to say to my nephew. Dorian Cartwright was the only part of my sister I had left. My only sibling died a few years prior in a car accident. Dorian resided with Colisa and me more and more through his teen years because we lived closer to his school.

The aroma of marijuana hit me as I approached his room. I knocked on the door a couple times with no reply. When I opened it, his back faced me. His head bobbed up and down as music thumped from his headphones. Light from the TV illuminated the room as he played video games. I grabbed his mp3 player and pressed pause.

He swung his head around to find out what happened to his music. A smile came across his face and he stopped his game. "What's up, Uncle Dre?"

He looks just like his momma. Nobody said 'Dre' like my sister except him. I inhaled the secondhand smoke and shut the door behind me. "That smells like some primo ganja you got there."

"It's pretty good stuff, Unc." He shifted around in his seat. "You should hit some. It might make your leg feel better."

"You know, I *would* if it was still back in the day." I grabbed the other controller out a nearby chair and had a seat. "Too Short and Gang Starr used to play when I sparked up the la-la. I stopped smoking because of my job. That's the only reason. What game is this you playin'?"

"This ain't no Pac-Man, Uncle Dre. It might be a little too much excitement involved." My nephew talked slick out the mouth, daring me to play. He pressed the button on his controller and focused on the TV. "It's called *Halo 4*."

"I'm sure that's a long way from Pac Man or Space Invaders. But that's not what I came in here to talk about." I placed the other controller on top of a stack of school books that were all worn out from my nephew's studies. A sense of pride hit me. "Congratulations again on getting your diploma early."

"I don't have the diploma yet, Uncle Dre. I won't get it 'til June like everyone else." Dorian spoke in a normal tone, but his body language and facial expression resembled that of a teenager deep into a video game. "I couldn't have done it without you and Aunt Lisa. Thanks."

"You're welcome." A smile came across my face. *This is a good dude.* "You give any more thought as to what you gone do now that high school is over?"

"I haven't made any decisions yet. Not really sure what I'm gonna do next." His eyes opened wide as he jerked the controller and his body to the left.

I stared at the TV in amazement at the quality of the graphics. "Yeah, this is a long way from Pong. Technology lost me after Ms. Pac Man."

He twisted the joystick to the right, then to the left. Next, he pressed multiple buttons as he frowned and bit his bottom lip. "You wanted to talk to me about something, Unc?"

Dorian sat with me on the porch during my Neighborhood Watch shift. It warmed my heart to keep a lookout with my sister's son at my side. I allowed him to spark up his weed one night so I could reminisce on the smell. That led to a second and third time. Soon, I let him spark up in his room while I sat there. I couldn't smoke, but the fragrance took me back and helped me relax at times. Apparently, he'd gotten more and more comfortable with smoking in the house. *But he's just a kid, and he ain't hurtin' nobody.*

"Ummmm, nah. I ain't got nothin' to talk about." My chest inflated as I took a deep breath and held it in for a few seconds. I came to my feet and spoke on my exhale. "Don't sweat anything, nephew. You've got your entire life ahead of you. Try to think about what you're gonna do next."

The TV lit up with several high-tech looking explosions. My nephew paused the game as he swiveled around to face me. "Okay, Unc. I think Aunt Lisa is mad at me. Maybe I should go stay at my father's house."

"She just had a bad day today." I sauntered to the door. "Don't worry about it. I'll talk to her."

Dorian's attention went to the video game as I exited his room. I moved down the hall to the master bedroom to rap with Colisa. The area was empty, so I strolled to Linda's room. I found my two ladies cuddled up on the twin sized bed fast asleep. A huge smile came over my face as they lay there peacefully. *Colisa makes being a mommy and a big girl so sexy.*

My adrenaline remained on ten from the night's excitement. In no way was I sleepy at that point, so I flipped on the TV in the living room and rested on a blanket along the couch. I caught a couple old episodes of *Rosanne* as I applied ointment and piled on a bunch of gauze from the medicine cabinet to my burns.

The clock struck 4 A.M. and the morning news played. The shooting at the Old School to New School Hip-Hop concert took off as the lead story on every channel. Kyle showed up as a witness on each network. One station flashed his stage name across the bottom of the screen and referred to him as a local Hip-Hop legend. They mentioned the fire on the roof of the garage and the name of our group a few times. The comments posted on Stallion Pee's social network page sealed him in as a primary suspect. The police held him for questioning. I checked out the coverage for at least an hour before dozing off.

The sun woke me up around 11 A.M. Colisa usually dropped the baby off at her mother's on Saturday mornings on the way to her bus route. I found myself in an empty house, except for my nephew. I tended to my burns and got some breakfast together. Dorian and I got our eat on in the kitchen as we watched the news. We learned the police released Stallion Pee.

The phone rang at exactly 12:16 P.M. I read the caller ID: *Antoinette Miller.*

Wow. We crossed paths the night before for the first time in years. She stormed onto the murder scene and wept over MC ET's corpse as he lay in his own blood. *I had no idea she was his mother.* Her presence at the murder scene caught me off guard. However, the phone call took me by surprise even more. *Why she tryna get up with me?*

I pressed the answer button on the phone and held it to my ear. "Hello?"

Chapter Five:
Antoinette Miller

May I speak with Andre Johnson, please?" The voice on the other ended slithered through the phone and into my head.

Nostalgia kicked in. Dozens and dozens of memories shot around my mind in one second flat. "This is he."

"Hi, Andre." The voice came off as trying to sound professional. "This is Nettie."

I knew exactly who the voice belonged to on the other end. No other soul knew about the nickname. I referred to her as 'Nettie' on exactly six occasions. After a second of silence, I said, "Hey."

Nobody said anything for three seconds.

"I got your number out the White Pages." She broke the silence. "You performed at the concert last night?"

"Yes. The shootings happened during our set." I didn't know where to start. "I'm so sorry about your loss. I didn't know he was your son."

"Thank you for the kind words. I didn't notice you last night, but I recognized your name while talking to one of the detectives."

Antoinette spoke in her work voice. "Did you see who killed my son?"

"Unfortunately, no, and I wish I did." I held the phone to my ear as I took a swallow of coffee. "Is there anything I can do to help?"

"I'm glad you asked." Her tone lightened up. "I need to find the truth. The police released the man they held in custody. So I called Doug. He wants to know if you can come to my house today and answer a few questions."

"Doug?" My mind paused a second due to the blast from the past. I got excited a little. "Doug from back in the day? Of course, I'll be happy to do whatever I can."

Doug Scott went to school with Antoinette and me. He never minded being called the token white guy when he hung with me and my people. He frequented black functions and events and fit right in without 'acting black.' Doug and I shared a dorm room sophomore year. We kicked it during meals, smoked together on a regular basis, and played chess all the time. He went on to become a police officer. Last time I heard from him, everything was everything.

"He will be here at three o'clock," she informed me. "Is that a good time for you?"

"Yeah, I'm free today." I grabbed a pen and an old envelope off the counter. "Where do you live?"

We disconnected the call after verifying the location a couple times. The cup of coffee sat on the kitchen counter as I stared at her address. I glanced up at a figure in the doorway. "Dorian?"

"It's me in the flesh, Uncle Dre." He stood there with a glass of juice in his hand. "Who was that?"

I paused for a few seconds. "Someone I went to college with. Turns out she's MC ET's mother."

"What?" He twisted his face and rested his glass on the table. "It's a small world, huh?"

"I know, right? I'm gone meet up with her and one of my boys today." I pivoted and leaned on the counter. "It's been a long time since I've seen either one of them."

"Can I go?" Dorian hung with me regularly and expected to tag along.

"Sorry, son." I took another swig of coffee. "It ain't the atmosphere for kids on this trip."

I warmed the truck and bundled up in layers. A 2010 silver and black Chevy Blazer rolled me across the South Side of Chicago. The radio thumped "I Left My Wallet in El Segundo" by a Tribe Called Quest. The sun shined brightly, but the temperature chilled at a cold twenty-seven degrees as I parked in front of Antoinette Miller's house. I stepped up her stairs and rang the doorbell. Steam rose from my nose and mouth and chills went down my body. A few seconds later, Doug opened the door. I cast my eyes upon my college homie. The skinny, athletic white dude with the baseball cap to the back grew into a thirty-something year old man. We slapped five as we gave each other a half-hug.

"What up, fam'? Five-O is in the house, huh?" I released Doug and stepped into the hallway as I joked with him. "What's with the goatee, old man? You gone pat me down before I come in?"

"I'm not a cop anymore." Doug brought me up to speed on his career path as he held the door open. "I'm a private investigator. I have a small office in Beverly."

That pleasantly caught me off guard as I took off my coat. "Okay, that's what's up. I see you're keeping in good shape."

"Oh, I try to do a little something a couple times a week." Doug shut the door behind me and eyeballed me from head to toe. "You still ain't no stranger to the gym yourself, huh? Still lookin' like Eric Sermon on steroids."

"You're tryna be funny, but I'm gone take that as a compliment." I wasted no time in asking about Antoinette. "Where is she?"

Wearing a white turtleneck style shirt under a dark gray suit jacket, Doug led me through a door into the living room. We stood around a spacious home that shouted urban working class. Lavender air freshener hit me in the nose.

Antoinette entered the area from the kitchen. As she strolled in, it felt like a spotlight shined on her and followed her along a red carpet. She got my attention with 5-foot 8-inches of high-yellow, curvy flesh that looked like it weighed in at just under two-hundred pounds. Her naturally curly hair hung just past her shoulders, with blonde streaks randomly scattered throughout her head.

Her voice quivered, and her eyes watered as she spoke. "It's good to see you."

"You too. I'm sorry it happened under these circumstances." I felt her pain as I moved in her direction to give her a hug.

We embraced for a few seconds in the middle of the floor. She welcomed me into her living room, so I parked it on the couch. Antoinette sat in a recliner as Doug paced the floor in front of us.

"I can't believe I'm looking at you two. It's been a minute. We should probably keep in touch more often." My eyes moved between Doug and Antoinette. "Y'all wanted to question me about last night, right?"

"Yes, what happened?" Antoinette asked as she leaned forward in her seat. "You okay?"

"I'm doing fine. Got a couple of slight burns, but it's cool," I said.

"Oh, I'm a nurse." Antoinette shared. "Are you taking care of it? Do you want me to examine it?"

"No, it's straight. But thanks for asking." It stung at that moment. I would've loved for her to give it some attention. "Why'd the police let go of Stallion Pee?"

"Because Stallion Pee has a major record label at his back with big time lawyers." Doug moved to the dining room table and sat behind a laptop. "I'm examining all the information the papers and the paparazzi have and seeing how much the police will share."

My thoughts shot to my conversation with Kyle. "Somebody showed me some messages Stallion Pee sent to the world via the Internet."

"They're gone." Doug brought that news to my attention. "All the statements he posted online last night have been deleted. His people released a statement saying someone hacked his account and sent those comments. Not him. Obvious quality control by his record company. They're protecting their new boy."

They deleted the messages? Instinct told me to speak up before he went any further. "Man, I don't know nothin' about no tweeps, twurps, or any of this new technology."

Antoinette and Doug chuckled.

"Don't lose any sleep on that." Doug flipped to the next page in his notebook. "However, we need to keep in mind that Stallion Pee and MC ET feuded on the Internet all the time. MC ET's last message to the world read: *#RegalTheater GSRA out back.*"

GSRA? More confusion set in. "And that means?"

"Not sure yet." Doug glanced between Antoinette and me. "But I'm working on it."

Antoinette fought back her tears. She rose and wandered past us. "I'm going to the kitchen to put on some coffee."

Doug probed me for information. "The police said you helped chase someone. Did you get a look at him at all?"

"No, I'm sorry. Through all the commotion, I never caught a glimpse of his grill."

"Besides Antoinette's son, there were two other casualties." His hand rubbed against his skinny chin. He gestured me to stand beside him. "It looks like all the shots fired came from the same gun. The cops discovered the same shell casings at each crime scene. Seventeen in all. So whoever did this probably got to the end of his clip. That's why he stopped shooting at you. He ran outta ammo."

I stood over Doug's shoulder. A picture of a man appeared on the screen. The person's information cascaded beside the photograph.

"The bodyguard shot in the alley went by the name of Edward Smith. He worked for the phone company during the day and had three kids." Doug read the profile information. He flipped to a different photo. "You already know DJ Roscoe P. Coltrane. Twenty-three years in Chicago radio. May he rest in peace."

"Definitely a tragic turn of events." My wheels rotated as I pieced the evening together. "MC ET and his hype man whipped Stallion Pee's ass right there in the backstage area. I saw it with my own eyes. That might explain why Stallion Pee would want to kill MC ET. But why would he want to pop DJ Roscoe?"

"That remains to be seen." Doug sat back in his chair. "The surviving bouncer spoke of a possible witness that observed the shooter fleeing. You remember seeing anyone?"

A *witness?* Everything happened so fast the night before. I recapped the events surrounding the shootings in my head again. "I don't remember any witness."

"You tagged along with the bouncers when they gave chase. Right?" Doug grabbed his pad and checked off notes with his pencil. "You guys noticed a young man at the bus stop wearing headphones."

"Wait." *Headphones?* A light went off in my head. "Right, ol' boy standing on the bus stop. Yeah, the young homie pointed us in the right direction."

"Another piece to the puzzle." Doug's eyes lit up.

I pulled a chair out and had a seat. "He rides the Number Nine all the time. I drop him off on 63rd and Ashland almost daily."

"This could be huge in shedding some light on the situation." Doug scribbled away on his notepad. "Approximately what time do you see him?"

"Usually weekdays in the early afternoon, right after lunchtime." I gave him all the information I knew of the young man. "He's short with kind of a round head. And he wears that Bears coat with those headphones all the freakin' time."

"Maybe he can identify Stallion Pee in a line-up." Doug made eye contact with me. "Keep this development between us right now. Don't get Antoinette excited until we know he'll cooperate."

I agreed we shouldn't get Antoinette excited. But that didn't stop *my* enthusiasm. It hit level ten as we discussed the evidence. I wanted to be more than a witness. *Maybe I can help solve this.*

The lady of the house returned on cue, carrying a tray with a pot of coffee and three empty mugs. Her eyes appeared even more bloodshot from crying. "Anything new?"

I hopped up and snatched the tray. "Let me get that."

"Stallion Pee is most likely to have done it, but he has a legal team in his pocket." Doug brought us up to speed on his intentions. "I'm gonna stay on him. From what I understand, he still hangs in the street. This is his first record deal, and he's close to messing it up."

I set the tray on the table and pulled out a seat for Antoinette. She pranced past me to the dining room window and opened the curtains to peeked outside. Her voice shook when she spoke. "Eric was my only child."

The afternoon sun shined through the openings in the blinds. She stood with her back to me, and I noticed a glow around her. Soft cries sounded off as she whimpered into a handkerchief. Memories of that cry hit my mind. I could tell she needed a shoulder to lean on. Doug fell into view and put his arm around her.

Jealousy kicked in. The emotions of a nineteen year old took over for a split second. Anger inside me wanted to snatch his arm off her and tell him to step back. I snapped out of my daydream. "I'm gone roll."

Antoinette hugged me as I expressed my condolences again. Doug walked me to the door and thanked me for the help as I put on my coat.

The possibility of solving an actual crime intrigued me to death. Real evidence needed to be examined. "Let me help with the investigation."

Doug smirked. "This ain't the college safety team, Andre."

The two of us joined student patrol at the same time when we became roommates. Most of the job consisted of walking female students from the library or the gym, back to their dorm rooms safely. We got to chase a thief or two here and there. And we fantasized about working a real case together one day.

"I know, and it's a dream come true." My eyes bucked open as my mouth watered. "You have your own private eye business? C'mon, man."

"Go home to your wife and kid, Andre." Doug opened the door and guided me out. "You gave a lot of great information. If I need you, I'll call you."

I retreated to the truck with my tail between my legs. The heat blasted in my face as I guided the ride to the house. I called Colisa to make sure she planned on being home for dinner, so I scooped up a family sized Giordano's deep dish pizza.

Colisa, Dorian, Linda, and I enjoyed family time until my baby girl got tired and fell asleep. Colisa and I watched a movie while Dorian played video games in his room.

The phone rang at 9:47 P.M., and the caller ID read: *Scott Investigations.*

I picked up the phone on the second ring and greeted Doug. "Hello."

He came straight out and told me the words I wanted to hear. "I need your help with the investigation."

Chapter Six:
Stallion Pee

Snow flurries hit Chicagoland the next morning, and two-inches of it stuck to the ground. I cleared the driveway and shared family time until noon. Colisa told me she had something planned for us at six, and I assured her I would return.

Doug asked me to meet him at Antoinette's place, and he instructed me to wear old gym shoes and sweat pants. He asked me to grab the oldest coat I had. We hooked up and went over the information at hand. He believed the only way to get the truth from Stallion Pee was to confront him face to face. Doug poked around on his computer and figured out his personal phone number. After getting no answer twice, Doug tracked his cell phone location to within six miles. He explained it to be easy for him if the person's phone is powered on.

This blew my mind. I marveled at how he opened a laptop and located another human being in twenty-three minutes flat. My fist wiped my eyes, and I gazed at the map on the computer screen. I didn't need any technology to recognize the six mile area covered gang territory along the Southside of Chicago. The Gangster

Disciples sold drugs heavily from three intersections within the highlighted area. Everyone in the city knew of these drug spots. However, the police never shut them down for some reason or another.

"We look the part." Doug dressed down himself in old jeans and raggedy gym shoes. He sat around the table with Antoinette and me. "This is the plan. We hit the drug spots one by one. Buy some rocks and ask a couple of loose ended questions to see if any of these clowns will tell us exactly where he is."

"I don't know if I can let you two do this." Antoinette stood up and leaned forward. "It sounds too dangerous."

"We got this." Doug reassured her as he rose from the table. "Don't worry. Everything is gonna be all right."

"Thank you both." She moved past the furniture to hug Doug. "You guys came right out without hesitation after all these years."

"It's all good." I held out my arms as she released Doug and came my way. "Don't worry. We gone figure out the truth. I promise."

She put her arms around my neck and pressed her body against me. My palms went from her waist to the middle of her back. Our cheeks rubbed against each other as we released.

I hopped in Doug's green 1996 Ford Escort with rear tinted windows. Rust covered the fenders as well as the front bumper, but the heat kicked like Bruce Lee. We approached the first drug spot and Doug pulled into a gas station. He slipped the car into park and eyeballed me.

"Okay, this is the deal." He adjusted his skullcap. "I need you to get in the trunk."

I thought this was a joke for a half second, but he looked serious. "What? I ain't gettin' in no trunk, homie. For what?"

"If you try to cop by yourself, this might work. If I try to cop by myself, we have a chance." He pushed the trunk unlock button, and it popped open behind us. "But if we roll through there together, they're gonna think we're cops."

"Oh, so why don't *I* drive and *you* get in the back." My way of thinking made a lot more sense to me.

"Can't do that. If something goes wrong, we don't want the record to show you buying rocks as you're sitting behind the wheel." He reasoned with me and hit me with some good logic. "That's gonna affect your driver's license and your job."

"Damn, man." I got out and made my way to the rear. "Don't mess around and lock me in this thing."

"Not gonna be a problem." Doug got out the driver side and met me. He lifted the hatchback. "You can pop right out through the seat if necessary. In fact, if I'm in trouble I'll say a key word. Watermelon. If you hear that, bust right through it. Use this if you need to."

My eyes popped open as Doug pointed to a sawed off shotgun that mounted the wall. We made eye contact for two seconds. I climbed in the tiny space, balled up into a comfortable position, and braced myself as he shut the lid.

Darkness surrounded me as his footsteps hit the concrete alongside the ride. The driver side door opened. The car sank as he sat down. It rattled as the door then slammed.

No heat back here. I bounced around as we pulled onto the street. We drove for a couple blocks and busted a left. After rolling for a few moments, we slowed down and stopped.

"We're at a stop sign." Doug spoke loud enough for me to hear him clearly. "I see somebody out here down the middle of the block. It's show time."

My heartbeat sped up a little. I braced myself as we pulled off. We hit a bump that made me bounce up and down twice. The burn on my leg smashed against the spare tire. *Shit!* I shook it off and ignored the pain as we slowed down.

"Park!" A male voice came from outside as we pulled over and stopped. The window cranked as Doug manually rolled it down.

The voice outside asked, "How many?"

"Two," Doug replied.

Silence rang out for a few seconds. The motor hummed and my body vibrated. Two small rays of brightness crept through an opening beside the rear lights. The shotgun rested above my head.

"Hey, y'all know Stallion Pee?" Doug's voice rang out from the front. "I want to get his autograph."

"What?" The voice outside shrilled off anger and confusion. "You asking questions about Stallion Pee? What are you? A cop?"

"No, I just like his music, and I heard he was Folks," Doug responded as he brought up Stallion Pee's affiliation with the Gangster Disciples. "I'm just showin' some love. I want the autograph before he blows up and leaves Chicago."

"What? Are you some type of reporter or something?" The voice paused and footsteps moved around outside. "Get on outta here, white boy. You got what you came for."

Multiple footsteps moved in on us.

Doug's voice got stronger. "I just wanna get this CD signed. I'll wait right here, man. You can take this to him and bring it right back."'

BAM!

Something banged against the other side of the ride.

What was that? I reached up and grabbed the shotgun.

"Rise up outta here, Opie Taylor. You been on the set too long," a different voice shouted from the passenger side.

Sweat came across my forehead. I lifted the shotgun from its mount and placed it in front of me.

Doug kept at them. "C'mon, man. Y'all can hook a fan up with an autograph. Right?"

"Heads up!" the thug yelled from the driver side.

Another soldier echoed the cry from a distance. "Heads up!"

C'mon Doug. This is nothing. Pull off, dog. I gripped the gun with one hand and placed my other hand on the rear seat.

"How y'all gone play me?" Doug spoke in a rejected voice. The vehicle jerked as the gear shifted. "I'm just trying to support some hometown rap music."

"Yeah, whatever. Just raise outta here, fool," the first thug's voice bellowed with authority.

The trunk bumped around as Doug drove away. We rolled for a minute and came to a stop before he spoke to me.

"Them dudes didn't wanna tell us anything." Doug pulled off and busted a right. "Let's hope we have some better luck at the next spot. I'm headed there now."

"No, uh-uh!" I shoved the seat forward. Light crashed into the trunk along with a bunch of warmth. I squinted as my eyes adjusted. "It's freezing back here, man. I gotta get out!"

I shoved the gun away and climbed forward into the seat. Doug drove around and pulled up at the same gas station we stopped at before.

"You all right back there?" Doug threw the vehicle into park and peeped over his shoulder to face me. "We certainly shouldn't give up just because we didn't get anything from *them*."

"I don't think this is gone get us anywhere." I rubbed my chin and glared out the window. "White boys can fall through here all the time to buy dope, but I don't see you gettin' too far askin' questions. Where the rocks at?"

"Right here." Doug grabbed two very tiny, light blue zip lock containers. He dropped them both in the palm of my hand. Obvious sarcasm followed. "What do *you* suggest, Mr. Know It All?"

"Just let me do it next time. If anyone's gone have any luck with this, it's gone be me." I examined the small, see-through plastic sacks filled with what looked like chipped off pieces of white soap. So much soap like substance stuffed the sacks that the zip lock part wouldn't zip together. Someone had to melt the edges shut to seal it. "Just drop me off around the corner from the next spot and stay nearby."

"That may not be a bad idea. Gimme your phone." He stuck his hand out in my direction.

"What? My phone?" I hesitated giving it to him. Why? I didn't know, because I barely used the thing. "What you want with it?"

"Just give it here."

I handed over the phone. Doug flipped it open and punched several buttons on it. He pulled out a small earpiece.

"Is that a bluetooth?" I asked as I stuck the rocks in my coat.

"Yeah." He pressed a button until a steady blue light beamed from it. Doug tapped the phone and both devices beeped at the same time. The steady light now flashed every four seconds. He handed me the earpiece and the phone. "Here, put this on and put your phone in your pocket."

Confusion sank in, but I followed Doug's instructions. I placed the earpiece over my ear and slipped the phone in my pocket.

"Can you hear me?" Doug spoke and his voice hit me in real time. The earpiece played it back about a second and a half later. *"Can you hear me?"*

"Wow, yes. How you do that?" It threw me how he spoke into thin air and it came through the headset. Meanwhile, my own voice did the same thing and caught me off guard as well. *"Wow, yes. How you do that?"*

"It's a microphone hanging from the sun visor." Doug pointed at a small black piece of plastic swinging over the front window.

I took off the headset before his voice traveled through. The heat made it comfortable as I closed the opening. "This muthafucka is raggedy, but you got it hooked up like a ghetto Batmobile. You just need some heat in this trunk."

He smirked and rolled off. "This baby gets me through stakeouts, and nobody ever looks at it twice. We will be able to stay in touch, but still be careful. These young bucks won't hesitate to pull the trigger."

"I realize that."

We moved on and pulled up a block before the next dope spot. I slipped on the bluetooth and hopped out the ride. Doug pulled off and drove an extra two blocks before making a left. The gloves went on as the wind rushed right through the old coat I dug out for the mission.

I pulled the hood over my head and tightened the string. The scarf went around my neck twice as I updated Doug. "It's cold."

"Hang in there, soldier," hit the headset. "You're from these parts, so I know you're used to it."

I curved the corner and strolled down the block. "It's funny, but I don't see anyone."

"It's nobody out there?" The empty block confused Doug, too.

"Not a soul. I would've thought there would be security out here at least." I spotted a man up the block. My breath appeared before my face when I spoke. "There's some dude up the street that looks like he's unloading groceries, but that's it."

"It sounds like it's not a lot going on." Doug picked up on my logic. "I'll just scoop you up, and we'll try the third spot. Maybe it's dry around here."

"Or maybe the block is just hot than a mug." My eyes bucked when a patrol car rolled onto the block. "Don't come scoop me. Five-O!"

"Okay, stay calm. You're clean, man." Doug went into police mode. "Don't panic. You don't have anything on you."

"Right." *Wait a minute.* I froze in my tracks. *Those rocks!* My heart rate sped up. "Hold up, man. I got that dope from the first spot on me."

"What?" Doug acted surprised. Sounds of him fumbling around took over the background. "What the hell are you doing with the rocks?"

"I forgot I had 'em!" I pulled the sacks out my pocket and took a quick peek to verify they were still there. "Shit, I'm dirty-than-a-mug out here!"

"Just relax." Doug tried to calm me down.

The cop car approached. I tucked in my chin and moved on down the block with my hands in my pocket. A gust of wind kicked in from the west as I changed directions and marched down the next walkway. Never looking back, I stomped toward the crib like I lived there. A soon as I hit the space between the houses, I peeked over my shoulder to verify I was out of the cop car's sight. Then I took off sprinting.

I dashed through the houses with the wind at my face. Luckily, who ever lived there put down salt that morning. I kept a steady pace until I reached the backyard.

"What's going on?" Doug's voice entered the headset.

Steam rose from my mouth as I huffed and puffed away. I squatted to the ground with my back against the house.

Doug tried to get my attention again. "You sound like someone's chasing you. I'm coming to find you."

"No!" I breathed heavily as I laid low and hoped the cop car passed without being nosey. "I think I lost them. Just chill for a minute."

I did my best to catch my breath as I remained still beneath a window. After several seconds, I noticed a female voice moaning and groaning. Soon, it hit me that someone nearby was having sex.

The voice groaned at a steady pace. "Oh, you a stallion, baby!"

Stallion? I came to my feet and stood on a crate to peep into a window with opened curtains and shades. The view went through a back porch that had been converted into a bedroom. The door opened to give me a perfect view of a bathroom. Stallion Pee stood in the shower having sex with a woman.

I couldn't believe my eyes as I whispered loud as hell, "Wait, hold up. We found the murder suspect!"

"What?" Doug's curiosity popped off. "Where?"

"I'm behind one of these houses. I just so happened to check the window . . . and there he is!"

"Sit tight. I'm on the way," Doug said.

Stallion Pee injected himself into the girl, doggy style. Her hands pressed the wall as she ducked her head beneath the stream of water. It shot down from the shower head and slammed against old boy's chest. Her voice sounded off in pleasure as he tapped her insides with aggression. He withdrew his dick and ejaculated all over the girl's ass and back. She moaned and groaned as he stroked himself with his hand. His semen dripped over the woman in globs.

He redirected the water flow from the showerhead as she turned and got on her knees. His penis entered her mouth and made her cheeks swell. She sucked and licked it up and down for a few seconds before he pulled it out. The female remained on her knees. He gripped his thing and leaned his head back.

My mouth dropped open in disbelief that we found him. The fact that we found him getting his groove on threw me even more.

His dick got more and more limp, and the girl stayed on her knees. I had no clue what they were waiting for until it happened. Liquid shot out dude's dong. At first I thought he came again. However, the fluid came out too fast and with too much force. It splashed the girl's neck and ran down her chest.

Oh shit! He's pissin' on her!

Stallion Pee released his urine all over the girl. He seemed to have the courtesy to not squirt her directly in the grill. She stuck her chin up as if to avoid pee getting on her face, but some of it splashed up there. The piss trickled off her body into the bathtub.

I see why they call him Stallion 'Pee.' No part of me wanted to witness these events, but for some reason I couldn't look away. I gagged, but caught myself before throwing up.

Once he finished, the girl came to her feet. Stallion Pee sat on his ass and stretched his legs out in front of him. The girl climbed up and placed one foot on each edge of the tub. The young man slid down into his own piss. The girl squatted and released her urine all over him. She squirted out more and more, and he sank right into it, smiling like he'd just won the lottery.

"Achoo!" I sneezed and lost my balance. The crate I stood on shook. I tumbled over and hit the ground.

WHAM!

Pain overcame my upper body.

The crate banged against the house.

"Who the fuck is that out there?" Stallion Pee's voice muffled behind the glass. Sounds of someone stumbling around approached the window.

I dragged myself to my feet and limped to the side of the house as fast as I could, keeping my back pressed against the freezing, hard bricks as I hid.

The window and the screen shot open. Stallion Pee's voice rang out loud and clear. "Who the hell is that out there!"

Thump, thump, thump!

I held my breath.

"Whoever it is, I got somethin' for you!" The window slammed shut. His voice muffled again. "It's too cold for this bullshit!"

Damn! My heart pounded away. *I'd better get outta here!* I took off up the gangway toward the front and darted into the front yard. As I stumbled around the corner, and I bumped into a 6-foot 4-inch, 215 pound goon.

The gangster pulled out a Glock and cocked it with his free hand. A bullet popped into the hole as he released.

CLICK!

He aimed it at my face.

My heart dropped. I froze in my tracks. *Shit!* I glanced around for the police. *Never around when you need them!*

The hood nigga stared daggers into me. "Where the hell you think *you* goin'?"

Chapter Seven:
Major League

My heart thrashed against my chest. Dude aimed the loaded gun directly in my face and grimaced as if I stole something.

"I'm not gone ask you again. Where you think you goin'?" Old boy's tone got stronger as he demanded an answer.

Panic almost overcame me.

Doug's voice came out of nowhere. "Tell 'im you're trying to buy a couple of rocks."

"What?" I forgot for a moment that Doug's ride connected to the bluetooth in my ear.

"I distinctly heard a gun cock, and somebody's asking you why you're there." Doug nailed the situation. "Tell him you're trying to buy drugs."

"Say *what* again, nigga! I dare you! I double-dare you!" The gunman's face tightened as he stepped toward me. "I don't like repeating myself!"

I raised my palms at him. "Whoa, whoa! I'm just lookin' for a rock!"

The guy stopped in his tracks. His weapon maintained a lock

on me. "Oh, you're on some crackhead shit? We done told y'all sad muthafuckas this ain't no dope spot no more!"

"Hey!" The door to the house burst open. A figure in sweat pants and a hoody stuck his body halfway out the door. "Who the hell is that?"

"It ain't nobody." The man with the gun directed his attention to the door as he kept his pistol pointed at me. "Just some old hyped-out nigga lookin' for a rock."

"Is that the fool who just looked though the back window?" Stallion Pee revealed his face as he squatted and shielded his eyes to get a better view.

"You peeped in the house through the window?" The goon lowered his gun as he eyeballed me. In the same motion, he cocked his left and drilled his fist into my chin.

WHAM!

My head jerked to the side and my body followed. I stumbled backward three steps and crashed dead on my ass in the snow. *Ah shit!*

The guard wiggled his hand like he hurt his knuckles.

"Bring his ass inside, Kool Breeze." Stallion Pee glanced around the area from left to right. "Hurry up. The block is hot."

Kool Breeze dragged me to my feet and guided me up the stairs. We crossed the front porch as I rubbed my chin.

"Don't panic, Dre." Doug's voice rang in my ear. "I can see them taking you in. Hang on. I'm gonna get you outta there."

"Watermelon would be good right now," I said to Doug, insinuating the obvious.

"Shut up!" Kool Breeze hushed me as he opened the screen and shoved me in. "Get yo' ass inside!"

"Okay, listen. They're gonna take the bluetooth away from you soon." Doug prepared me for the inevitable. "Look around and pay attention to everything. Don't talk if you don't have to, and don't touch anything. Just give short answers and be—"

"What's this?" Stallion Pee snatched the headset off my ear. "You got a bluetooth? Get yo' dumb ass over there and get on the floor."

Kool Breeze guided me through the living room area. An old dark green couch sat against the wall near a glass table surrounded by several folding chairs. Playing cards lay scattered on it randomly. He used his revolver to nudge me into an unfurnished dining area. I dropped to the scuffed floor. Stallion Pee placed the headset to the hardwood and crushed it with his heel.

"Who are you? Some type of reporter or something?" he questioned as he took a good look at my face. "Hold on . . . wait a minute. I know this dude."

I posed with my palms spread to the sky. The heat in the crib crept through my clothes as it erased the chill from outside. I frowned and held my chin high.

"Yeah, I know this cat. It's one of those old school niggas." Stallion Pee put two and two together to figure out my identity. "Yeah, he was at the show the other night. It's one of the MC's from Inner City Youth."

I smiled. *He recognized me from my Hip-Hop crew. That's what's up.* I lowered my arms some.

He looked me up and down. "Y'all should change the name of the group 'cause it's twenty years later. Inner City Youth? Y'all look more like Suburban Old Men."

Kool Breeze laughed as he aimed the Glock at me.

I got pissed a little bit. That marked the third time I'd heard that joke in the previous two weeks. My hands lowered some more.

"You around here in nineteen degree weather tryna cop a rock?" Stallion Pee frowned as if he tasted a sour lemon. "Damn, homie. You on this shit that bad?"

I got offended. My eyebrows crumpled for two seconds, and then it hit me. *He thinks I'm a hype.* I scratched my neck with both hands similar to Tyrone Biggums, the drug addict on the *Dave Chappelle Show.*

"Look at him, man." Stallion Pee spoke to Kool Breeze as he kept his eyes on me. "Keep him covered while I pat him down."

I stuck my hands out as he came over and checked me for weapons. Surprisingly, he didn't smell like pee. He must've gotten up on some soap and water after the piss party.

"He's clean." Stallion Pee strolled away from the dining area and through the kitchen. An empty counter divided the two rooms. "Put that gun away and keep an eye on him."

Kool Breeze lowered the gat to his side and smirked at me.

My face throbbed as I returned his stare. *This nigga stole on me.* I rubbed my grill as I sized him up.

"Ol' girl just bounced." Stallion Pee returned through the kitchen carrying two baseball bats. Glass cabinets hung over a sink. "Get rid of that piece, fool! I ain't tryna get caught around it. I don't know why you grabbed it for this clown, anyway."

"I heard him runnin' back and forward between the houses." Kool Breeze marched the weapon into the living room, away from my sight. "This fool could've been another crazy and confused Vice Lord."

"True, and nobody's on street level right now." Stallion Pee positioned one of the bats against the wall.

"Somebody's unloading groceries." Kool Breeze's voice sailed in from the living room. "Other than that, it's quiet on the front."

"That's how this fool slipped through." The other bat swung in the air as Stallion Pee took a couple of practice swings. He focused on me as he spoke about me in third person. "This hype got caught in the wrong place at the wrong time."

Kool Breeze strolled into the dining area empty-handed. "You gonna let him go? Or kill him?"

My attention level shot to a hundred.

"Nah, I ain't gone kill 'im. Even though he's a fuckin' hype, he'll probably be missed." The tip of the bat hit the ground as Stallion Pee leaned on it. "But we're gonna beat his ass for invading my privacy."

Oh shit!

A devious grin came across Kool Breeze's face. He giggled an evil laugh and grabbed the bat against the wall. "This ought to be fun."

They gripped the bats like Major League Baseball players. Kool Breeze's big-ass resembled a left-handed Frank Thomas from the White Sox. Stallion Pee's skinny, dark-skinned frame matched Alfonso Soriano from the Cubs if you overlooked the dreadlocks.

Thump! Thump! Thump!

My chest banged, and perspiration collected under my armpits.

Kool Breeze poked at me with the weapon. The tip of the bat crashed into my shoulder.

I flopped to the floor.

"Get up, fool!" Stallion Pee yelled.

A sharp pain took over my arm and ached surprisingly more than anticipated. I glanced at the two gangbangers surrounding me on either side. The big one growled as he gripped the bat with one hand. The younger one tapped the barrel of the billy club on his palm.

BAM! BAM! BAM!

Someone banged on the front door.

BAM! BAM! BAM!

Both thugs bent their knees and expressed an air of fear.

"Who the fuck is that?" Stallion Pee stared at Kool Breeze.

"Open up! It's the police!" A voice from outside snatched everyone's attention.

"Oh shit! Five-O! Gimme the bat." Stallion Pee grabbed the club from Kool Breeze's hand. He took off toward the rear, whispering loud as hell. "You put that piece away?"

"Yeah, it's in the wall," Kool Breeze whispered loud in return as he stood over me. "The cops are here? Why?"

BAM! BAM! BAM!

The door banged some more. The voice from outside yelled, "Open up!"

Stallion Pee stormed in from the back and tossed a set of brass knuckles to Kool Breeze. "Grab his ass and take 'im downstairs. If he makes a peep, bust him in his skull until he passes out."

No! My adrenaline flew into high gear.

Kool Breeze dragged me to my feet.

WHAM!

The front door thumped.

WHAM! WHAM!

The three of us posed in the middle of the dining room with confused expressions on our faces.

WHAM!

The front door flung open on a final kick.

"Freeze! Nobody move!" Doug stormed in holding a badge and pointing his pistol across the room. "Hands! Lemme see your hands!"

I jerked away from Kool Breeze's grip as his palms shot to the sky.

Stallion Pee put his arms straight in the air. "Is there a reason for the intrusion, officer? You bustin' in here like you got a warrant."

"Shut up and jiggle those fingers!" Doug put the badge in his pocket and gripped his piece with both hands. He aimed it at Kool Breeze. "Put down the brass knuckles! Drop it before I drop you!"

Kool Breeze released the weapon, and it thudded to the hardwood.

"You two, move into the living room!" Doug pointed his weapon and ordered the GDs to go in one direction. He nodded at me to go the opposite way. "*You*, get over there."

I rubbed my shoulder and ignored Doug's commands. Steam shot from my ears as I sized up Kool Breeze. He posed between the folding chairs. *This nigga hit me in my face.* I inhaled and stomped in his direction with an inflated chest. My fist exploded into his chin.

WHAP!

Kool Breeze flew backward off his feet and rammed into the top of the table.

CRASH!

Glass shattered in several directions. The table legs collapsed as he tumbled the rest of the way to the floor and lay there motionless.

"Don't!" The shout from Doug came a little too late.

"Are y'all serious?" Stallion Pee's palms went down half way and faced upward as he questioned Doug in disbelief. "Wait a minute. Is *he* a cop, too?"

"Shut up!" Doug kept the firearm aimed at Stallion Pee and waved him toward the kitchen. "Keep your hands up and move. Don't make me shoot!"

Stallion Pee cooperated. His hands shot above his head as he arrived at the entrance to the kitchen area. He stopped beside the counter and glanced at me. "You're five-O, too? Lemme see *your* badge."

"I ain't got no damn badge." I marched in his direction with my fist balled. "Suburban Old Men, huh? I oughta bust you in your chops, you skinny little—"

"Whoa, slow down, cowboy." Doug intercepted me with his free hand as he kept the nine on Stallion Pee. "Relax while I ask the young rapper a couple of questions right quick."

"I don't know what y'all want, man." Stallion Pee showed little fear as he posed at the edge of the kitchen. "I'm clean, and this house is clean."

"What happened when Inner City Youth took the stage the

other night?" The question floated from Doug's mouth.

"Huh?" Stallion Pee hit us with a look of shock. He frowned and dropped his arms to his side. "Is that what y'all sweatin' me for? Y'all can just talk to my lawyer about that."

"Keep those hands where I can see them!" Doug put bass in his voice and tried to intimidate the young artist.

He showed no fear. "So that's what this is about. I'm gone tell y'all again. My crew went to our bus when they kicked everybody out the building, and that's where we remained until after the shots fired. All of us."

"I need you to get those hands up!" Doug's voice escalated some more.

"Sorry, can't do that." His eyes scanned from my eyes to Doug's. "You niggas ain't cops."

Uh-oh! That caught me off guard. Doug lowered his weapon slightly.

"First of all, five-O wouldn't bust in here without evidence and without back up. I know there's no proof against me, because I didn't do it." Stallion Pee crossed his arms and rubbed his chin. He glanced at me, and then pointed in my direction with his thumb. "Secondly, this fool ain't got no badge. And I believe if I ask to see your badge again, it won't happen. Plus, the real cops are being too careful. They don't want to fuck up."

He's figuring us out. I glanced at Doug as he glanced at me. His piece lowered some more.

"So the way I see it, you two are trespassing. That leaves me only one choice." Stallion Pee pivoted one hundred-eighty degrees. He leaped in the air with his hands in front resembling Superman as he gave his command. "Shoot 'em!"

POW! POW!

Shots rang out from behind us.

We ducked. Bullets whizzed by us and shattered the glass cabinets.

CRASH! CRASH!

Glass flew in every direction. I turned and caught Kool Breeze aiming his weapon at us. *Shit!* Doug and I leaped in the air and flew over the counter head first at the same time.

POW! POW! POW!

More shots filled the air.

We crashed into the floor on the other side of the counter as bullets ricocheted around the kitchen. Glass scattered around us. I tumbled into the fridge and pushed myself against the counter. Stallion Pee sprung to his feet and bolted toward the back door.

Doug came to a squatting position. He grabbed his weapon with both hands and took a deep breath. His knees thrust his body just enough to aim the Glock over the counter. Doug's eyes bucked open. "He's gone!"

I came to my feet and saw an empty living room and a vacant dining area. By reflex, I took off in Kool Breeze's direction. "I'm going after 'im!"

"No!" Doug caught my attention as he ran the opposite way. "Forget about him. Let's get Stallion Pee!"

I followed as he busted out the rear of the house. Stallion Pee darted through the backyard and sprinted down the alley. Doug and I sprung over all the stairs and landed safely on the concrete. We gave chase.

Stallion Pee scampered through the alley. His breath floated in the air similar to steam coming from a locomotive. He whisked down the passageway with a five building lead and broke in between two garages.

Doug flew along the alley and stayed on his trail. I swung in between two nearby garages with hopes of cutting him off at the pass. Halfway down and adjacent to the structure rested a six-foot fence. I hopped in the air and grabbed the gate with both hands. My foot hit the top. I thrust myself over and landed on one foot as I easily maintained my stride.

As soon as I crossed the end of the garage, an angry pit bull sprinted my way.

"ROOF! ROOF! ROOF!"

I paused like a deer staring into headlights. *Oh shit!*

The dog used all its might to shove off its hind legs. Its powerful front limbs grabbed the ground as it charged in my direction. Each stride brought my doom closer.

"ROOF! ROOF!"

I sprung in the direction of the yard next door and grabbed the top of the gate.

The dog's teeth caught hold of the bottom of my sweat pants as it tried to pull me down. Muscles flexed on the dog's body and it used its legs to gain leverage.

"GGRRRRR!"

My fingers and one foot latched to the fence. I gritted my teeth and frowned as I tugged away from the canine.

RIIIIIP!

The elastic in my pants gave way around the ankle. Momentum caused the dog to stumble backward.

I pulled myself to the top of the gate, leaped to the other side, and tumbled to the ground.

The dog rushed the gate and barked at me with all its might.

"ROOF! ROOF! ROOF!"

Wow! I came to my feet. The dog barked away along the gate as I exited the yard and jogged to the front of the crib. I saw Doug in someone else's yard about five houses down. We surveyed the area but saw no signs of Stallion Pee. Doug frowned and shrugged with his palms toward the sky.

A police siren faded in from a distance. Doug and I met halfway.

"He got away." Doug's breath appeared in the air as he bent over and grabbed his knees.

"Man, I drive for the City of Chicago." Panic came over me. "I can't be caught up in no trespassing nonsense."

"Let me handle the cops." Doug stood upright. "You get outta here."

"Where am I supposed to go?"

"Meet me at Antoinette's place." He stood upright. "Cut through the yard across the street and don't look back. Take the bus and meet me there."

"What about these rocks?" I reached in my pocket and held them out in front of us.

"I'll take care of this." He grabbed them and stuck them in his pocket. "Don't worry about me. Just go. I'm good with the cops."

We split, and I cut across the street without looking over my shoulder. I stomped through yards and crossed four streets until I got to the nearest bus stop. The wind picked up and shot chills through my body as the bus pulled around. I thanked the lord the driver didn't know me as I swiped my back pocket along the fare reader.

Beep.

I sat in the farthest seat in the back on the right side of the bus. Nine other passengers minded their own business talking on cell phones, reading books or staring out the window. I hoped Doug had everything under control. Two transfers later, I got off on Antoinette's block. I sneezed three times as I tightened my muscles and double-timed it up the street. My body shivered in the cold as I rang her doorbell.

She opened the door wearing a pink fitted long sleeve T-shirt with no bra. Pajama bottoms and big furry house shoes put her comfort appearance on ten. Her nipples poked out through her top. *She's still big, juicy, and curvy. Just like I like 'em.*

Her body shivered as she held the door open. Using a seductive voice, she said, "Please, come in."

Chapter Eight:
Hot Toddy

I ducked in out the cold.

"Where's Doug?" Antoinette shut the door behind me. "Is he okay?"

"Yeah, he's fine. We found Stallion Pee and talked to him, but the cops came." I brought her up to speed as we faced each other in the foyer. "Doug told me to break camp, and he stayed behind."

"Why?" She covered her mouth with her hand. "What happened?"

"We made a little too much noise while we spoke to him." I didn't want to tell her about them shooting at us. *No need to upset her.* "Unfortunately, there's nothing new to report."

"I've been waiting to hear from you guys." Her son's death weighed heavily on her face. She led me to her living room, and then shut the door to the hallway. "Do you think he killed Eric?"

"I watched Doug question that kid," I said as I recalled Stallion Pee's confidence in denying anything to do with the murder. "It's still hard to tell. There's really no hard evidence against him right now."

Her eyes watered a little. She crossed her arms and brought on the sad face that I became so familiar with long ago. Antoinette's lips poked out, and she sobbed while her left eye twitched. She shivered away. "You brought the cold in with you."

"Let me generate you some heat." I kicked off my shoes, took off my coat, and then rubbed the outside of her arms.

"Achoo!" I sneezed in both palms.

"This weather seems to be catching up with you." She strolled to the kitchen. "I'll fix you a hot toddy."

I staggered over and eased onto her lime green couch. Agonizing pain throbbed in my shoulder as I attempted to switch to relaxation mode. *This is a bit more than I expected.* The burn stung at a steady pace. As much as I hated it, I needed to let someone examine it.

"Achoo!"

"Just what the doctor ordered. One hot Theraflu with a shot or two of Old Grand Dad." Antoinette returned with a tray and set it on her coffee table. "It's the same whiskey my grandmother used to knock the cold from my cousins and me when we were kids."

I turned to face her. A sliced orange and a bottle of Nyquil accompanied the drink. Steam rose and hit me in the nose. I took a sip. My lips tightened, and I hummed my approval. "This actually hits the spot."

"How's your leg doing?" She made herself comfortable beside me. "I almost asked you this yesterday. Are you still afraid of hospitals?"

"I'm not *afraid* of anything." The medicine and alcohol warmed my chest as I set the mug on the table. "But it may be time to let a doctor look at this burn, indeed. This baby stings."

"I've been working for the University of Chicago for almost twenty years now. I'm a nurse. Remember?" She reached toward my limb. "Here, let me see it."

"Ouch!" I yanked away before she could touch me. My ass slid down the couch. "No, thank you. What you tryin' to do to it anyway?"

She laughed under her breath. Her tone adjusted as if she spoke to a four-year-old child before getting school shots. "I just wanna take a quick peek at it. Okay? I promise I won't touch it."

Her soothing voice earned my trust. Either that, or the pain demanded the nearest available attention. I raised my pants to show off a leg with an Ace bandage wrapped around it. I unrolled the outer covering and revealed a large Band-Aid style bandage over the worst burn.

"Oh no, sugar. That's too much." Antoinette's eyebrows came together, and she shook her head. "You're not supposed to wrap it up like that. You gotta let it breathe, so it can heal properly.

The air hit my wound as I peeled off the last Band-Aid. I winced as the largest of several lesions throbbed away.

"It could definitely be worse." Antoinette came to her feet and then squatted to get a closer look. "Yep, first degree burns. You can get away without going to the doctor if you take care of it correctly. C'mon."

"Oh, anything that will save a trip to the hospital," I said.

She led me down the hall to the bathroom and ran some water in the tub. A first aid kit came out the linen closet along with a set of white towels. "Rinse your wounds off under the cool water for a little while."

I kicked off my shoe and sock, and then stuck my foot in the tub. The water hit me and brought some relief to the burns. My upper body throbbed. *I can't let her know how much pain I'm in.* Antoinette stepped away and moved about her home. The clock read 8:45 P.M. *Shit! I was supposed to meet Colisa at six! This ain't good!* Tension already kicked it in my house too much those days. My brain raced about the argument waiting for me at home.

Antoinette returned in ten minutes. "Does it feel okay?"

"Yeah, actually, it does. I could hold my leg under this faucet forever." I didn't want to move, but my wife and kids hit the forefront of my mind. "I appreciate you trying to take care of me, but I'm not sure I can go on with the investigation. I gotta go."

"What?" Antoinette's face went into shock. She froze in her tracks and grabbed her chest. "Why?"

"I wanna figure out who did this to your son, but I don't think I have the time to invest." I truly wanted to help, but my wife had been on me about a lot of things. My heart anticipated me being in a position to have to make up lost time. "I'm sorry. But it's nothing personal."

"But you and Doug make a good team. I called him right away when I learned you were involved." She pleaded her case well. "Nobody else is gonna care enough to investigate as hard as you two. I already know what you guys are capable of."

"Believe me, I sympathize." Of course, the chance to help find her son's killer thrilled me. Working with Doug brought me more excitement than I'd seen in a long time. But I knew better. "I want to help, but I can't promise anything."

Her expression went from disappointment to anger. But then it changed into a devious smile. She handed me a towel with one hand and turned off the water with the other. "I understand. At least let me finish taking care of you."

"Thank you." I dried off. "You have anything for the pain?"

"Funny you should ask," she said with a crooked smile. "I do indeed have something *just* for you."

I moved to the living room. She went in the other direction as the fireplace heat hit me. I kicked back and dried off some more.

Antoinette returned to the room and placed a pill organizer divided into four sections on the TV tray. She pointed at the container. "Here's something for your pain. These are aspirin and these are ibuprofen. These other ones over here are prescription

Vicodin. One of those should be more than enough to make you feel better."

The three sections she described contained blue pills. I pointed to the fourth area she ignored. "What about the big red ones?"

"That's *way* stronger than Vicodin. That's the stuff they let the astronauts play with." She exited the living room, switching her ass cheeks left to right. "You don't need anything *that* strong. Take your pick."

If you only knew about the pain in my shoulder. As soon as she strolled out of sight, I grabbed a red pill and popped it in my mouth. It dissolved on my tongue like an Alka Seltzer. My mouth shot off like I'd eaten a handful of Pop Rock Candy. It got pretty intense before I chased it down with the hot toddy, which was more of a room temperature toddy by then.

Antoinette returned wearing latex gloves. She carried a long Q-tip and a silver tube with a prescription label on it. "This will help it heal a bit faster."

I stretched out to give her a good angle. The ointment soothed the burn somewhat. She lightly wrapped my lower leg with gauze and placed a small piece of white tape on it. It didn't feel all confined anymore.

Soon, the pain vanished. "That pain killer's kickin' in quite nicely."

"You can feel it, huh?" She approached me and stared deep into my pupils. "I would have to agree. Looks like it's kicking in all right . . . all right . . . all right."

What the— Her voice echoed and faded away, yet her lips didn't move. My grill tightened up. Muscles I didn't even know I had in my face flexed. "I'm feeling a little funny. My mouth feels clammy."

Antoinette grabbed the pill organizer and the TV tray. She strutted to the rear bedroom. The walls closed in from every direction, and then bounced outward. I grabbed my face to make sure it was still there. My eyes closed, and I shook my dome in circles. Footsteps banged like a drum and echoed in my head like I was in a long tunnel. I opened my eyes and caught Antoinette approaching me. She grabbed my hand and pulled me to my feet. Her body pressed against mine.

It felt good; but *way* beyond any type of regular good. Something wasn't right, but the way she touched me sent bolts of tingling electricity from head to toe unlike anything I'd ever experienced.

She gazed at me. Her facial features appeared sharper, and she had a glow about her. Antoinette pressed her face against mine and whispered in my ear, "I need you to help me find my son's killer . . . killer . . . killer . . . killer."

Whoa! Her voice echoing amazed me, and the warmth from her breath sent chills through me. I put my palm on her back. "I'm gonna get to the bottom of this. I promise."

She didn't let go. My mind wanted her to release me, but my body buzzed as if someone activated a continuous orgasm in me. An erection throbbed through my sweat pants. She shoved me onto the couch and pulled them down.

Oh my God! Every nerve in my body tingled as her mouth slid up and down my rod. I reached an unbelievable level of sensation when she climbed on top of me and slid down the rock. The couch squeaked as our thrusts met in the middle. She rode me into the night. We held each other tight as I shot off inside her with all my might. Something so wrong felt so physically unbelievable. My flesh melted every time my skin touched hers. The sensation continued as we held each other.

The feeling finally peaked, and the tingling subsided. A tear ran down my cheek as I tried to move. Extreme exhaustion took over. Dizziness overwhelmed me, mixed with fatigue. I couldn't keep focused as I grew detached from myself and my physical surroundings. I floated in the air and watched myself lying in

Antoinette's arms. Everything went black.

*****

My eyes popped open at 3:27 A.M. Antoinette rested on my arm as we slept awkwardly with every light in the house still on. We both had on our tops, but we checked in naked from the waist down.

I shoved her off me and came to my feet. "Oh my God! What have we done?"

She woke up and glanced around the room like she didn't know where she was.

"How did this happen!" I had no memory of having sex with this woman. My head banged out of control, and it got worse when I yelled. I lowered my tone. "Jesus Christ, Nettie. I'm married. I've never cheated on my wife before."

Antoinette swung her legs around and sat up. She glanced up at me, covered her face, and cried me a river.

"I know we didn't just do what it looks like we did." Dried semen and vaginal secretion along my private parts proved differently. *No!* I'd never felt that sluggish in my entire life. I paced the floor from left to right. "What am I gonna do?"

Ding, dong!

The doorbell rang out.

The two of us frowned and stared at each other.

"Are you expecting company?" I asked.

Ding, dong!

The bell rang again, and the front door opened.

Doug's silhouette strolled into the foyer area. "Hello?"

Oh shit! I grabbed my pants, shoes, coat, and underwear, and then ran in place.

Antoinette slipped on her pajama pants and whispered loud as hell, "Behind the couch!"

I tipped across it with my naked ass showing and my clothes in hand. Antoinette stumbled into her house shoes and went toward the front door. I spotted one of my gym shoes smack dead in the middle of the floor. *Damn it! Too late to grab it.*

"Did you know you left your door open?" Doug entered the living room.

I ducked all the way down and hid from his view.

"No, I didn't." Antoinette's voice shook at first, but she gained control of her nerves. "Thank God it's you and not some criminal."

"I know, right? Where's Andre?" Doug's voice got stronger as it moved in my direction. "He should've been here hours ago. His car is still outside."

"You tell me. Weren't you two together?" Confusion came through Antoinette's voice. "What happened with the case? Did you talk to Stallion Pee?"

"We found him, but we didn't get anything." Doug flopped down on the couch. He spoke to Antoinette as he rested only a few inches away from me. "More importantly, I'm worried about Andre. He should've been here a long time ago."

"Maybe you should go back and try to find him?" She tried to give him a reason to leave. "He could need your help."

"I've been calling his phone for hours with no answer." Concern burst through his voice. "The best thing for me to do right now is to just stay put on this couch right here, to see if he shows up."

Damn! I hunched over a few inches away on all fours with no pants or shoes on. Doug brought Antoinette up to speed with a watered down version of the investigation. She attempted to get him to leave the room several times, but he didn't give in.

At one point she got him to take a look at her computer. As he got up, she dropped my other gym shoe over the couch. It landed on my back. I grew uncomfortable as Doug returned and sat down. He decided to take the conversation in a different direction.

"I'm glad we're alone like this, Antoinette." The couch moved as Doug repositioned himself. "There's something I want to tell you. I want us to get back together."

"What? Wow, Doug. Maybe this isn't the best time to bring this up." She stood up. "There's a lot going on right now. Plus, we haven't seen each other in years."

"So what? And are you kidding? This is a *great* time to talk about this." Doug came to his feet. "It was awesome being with Andre today. And it feels good being next to you again. These are terrible circumstances, but I'm reunited with my best friend and my favorite girl."

Doug and Antoinette kicked it big time during school. In fact, I met Antoinette through Doug. Their relationship lasted most of the four years we spent at Northern. They even shacked up toward the end of school and were practically engaged. They broke up and got back together exactly five times throughout college. Antoinette and I got our freak on once during each of those break ups.

Guilt overcame me as my joints throbbed. My ass caught a chill as it stuck in the air, plus an old Chuck Taylor rested on my back.

"Listen, I'll talk about this with you, but only if you come to the kitchen with me." She finally said something to get him to move. "C'mon. Let me make you a hot toddy while we wait for Andre to show up."

Their footsteps faded out the room. I came up and peeped over the couch. Their voices remained in the kitchen as I slipped on my pants and tipped across the floor. I stuck my drawers in my pocket and put the remainder of my clothes on in the foyer area. Antoinette spoke extra loud and banged pots and pans around as a distraction. I peeled open the front door and stepped into the cold. Ten seconds later, I rang the doorbell as if I just showed up.

"You just get here?" Doug rushed the door and bombarded me with questions. "Are you okay?"

"Yeah, man. I fell asleep riding the Green Line. Woke up and I found myself on an empty train with the lights out sitting at Harlem and Lake." The lie danced from my mouth without skipping a beat. I knew not to spend a lot of time on it. "What the cops say?"

"It's all good. My gun never fired a single shot." Doug peeped over his shoulder as we posed in the foyer. "I scooped up the bluetooth pieces and ducked away before the police arrived. I ended up connecting with my old partner for a few hours. Come on in, so I can fill you in with the details."

"Nah, man. I've got to get home to the family." Shame sunk in as I mentioned my wife and kids. I grew frustrated because I couldn't remember anything from the time I held my foot under the bath water, until the time I woke up half naked. "Tell Antoinette I said good night."

I gave Doug some dap and sat in the truck until it warmed up. My mind raced out of control as I tried to recall what went down between Antoinette and me that would put us in that position.

Just before sunrise, I pulled into the driveway of the crib. The home belonged to me along with Colisa, Linda, and Dorian. That night, I disgraced them all. I let the door down on the connecting garage and entered the house. The moment I went in the dining room, I sensed someone else's presence.

The light came on, and Colisa sat at a table set for two looking extra pissed. An opened bottle of wine rested near her with only about an inch of liquid left at the bottom. Wax stuck to the sides of candleholders that housed candles that burned to the lowest point. She wore the red nighty I loved. It fell nicely over her thick curves.

Colisa rose and leaned forward. Her eyebrows wrinkled. "How could you?"

Chapter Nine:
Colisa Garrett-Johnson

*T*humph! *Thump! Thump!*

My heart raced out of control. *She knows!* I froze, paralyzed and speechless.

"I don't believe it!" Colisa twisted her lips and sat down in her seat. "No, wait a minute. I believe it. I *completely* believe it. This is typical Andre as of late."

"I apologize; I don't know what happened." *How do I explain this?* I set my keys on the table as my head banged away. My palms faced the sky. "I didn't mean for it to go down like this. I'm sorry, baby."

"You're sorry? Yeah, your ass is sorry, all right." She grabbed her half-full glass of wine and posed in her seat with it before she took a sip. "I trusted you!"

Guilt and nervousness fought in my stomach, and it resulted in butterflies. My hands shook as I stood there imagining the consequences of my actions. *I've lost her this time. There's no excuse for what I've done.*

"You were supposed to be home at six." She raised one

eyebrow and rolled her neck. "I didn't know that I had to specify AM or PM."

"There's really no excuse." I couldn't justify to myself why I'd slept with Antoinette. No way could I justify it to Colisa. "You have every right to be upset with me."

"Damn right!" She set her glass on the table and shoved the chair behind herself as she came to her feet. "I don't ask you to do too much. Be home at six this one time. That's all."

My eyes opened wide. *Wait, she doesn't know ... yet.*

"And if you weren't gonna make it, all you had to do was pick up the phone." She moved around the table and stepped in my direction. "I called your little tired-ass flip phone twice, and it went straight to voicemail."

I felt around at my waist. *Where the hell is my phone?* My hand went into the pocket of my sweat pants, and grabbed onto my underwear. *Oh shit! My drawers are in my pocket!*

"What happened? You went to play cops and robbers with your friends?" She approached me with one hand on her hip. "What happened this time? Did you get shot at again?"

Wow. No way could I let her know that, that happened. More importantly, she moved closer and closer to me. *Damn it! I'm not fresh!* I spun away from her and strolled to the kitchen. "You're right. You don't deserve what I've put you through."

"What about work?" She followed me. "You have to be there in three hours."

That's right! I got so caught up in the recent events that I forgot the vacation was over. "I'm calling off."

"What's gotten into you?" She slapped me on the back. "Don't walk away from me!"

Frustration kicked in, and I grew more sluggish and lethargic. However, I couldn't let this situation escalate, because we faced even bigger issues. I turned and faced her. "Look, a lot happened today. I know I should've called, but I lost my phone in all the commotion."

Colisa shifted her weight to one leg and stared at the ceiling as she shook her head. "Do I even wanna know what happened?"

No! I kept space between us as I looked away. My peripheral vision caught her staring a hole in me.

"The Neighborhood Watch is one thing. I look at that as an excuse to hang out and drink beer with the people on the block." With one hand on her waist and the other hand pointing at me, she expressed herself. Her voice lightened up and showed concern. "But you were shot at the other night, Andre. What about your family?"

She's right. Taking a step back, I realized I needed to defuse the situation. I glanced around the kitchen. "My bad. You know I would never intentionally do anything to hurt you and the kids. I certainly didn't know you planned to do all this."

A glass lid covered the big pot on the stove. From the smell alone, I knew oxtail stew rested inside.

"I made your favorite dish tonight." Her eyebrows went up, and she crossed her arms.

And it was my favorite dish, indeed. Again, I inhaled the familiar scent. My mother made it for me as a kid, and she shared the recipe with Colisa before she passed away. "What's the occasion?"

"I wanted to spend some time with you. We haven't had a quiet moment together since you decided to do these shows." Colisa took a step in my direction. "I'm just trying to spend some time with my husband."

"Yeah, I know I haven't been around over the last couple weeks. And I've missed you." My arms fell to my sides, and I leaned in to meet her for a hug. *Wait! Nigga, you smell like another bitch's coochie!* My knees collapsed, and I squatted to the floor as I grabbed my ankle. I limped away from her real fast. "Ow! The leg! Ouch!"

"What's wrong? Is it the burns?" She came behind me to try to help.

No, don't follow me! I scurried to the kitchen table and pointed her off. "The alcohol! Can you grab it out the bathroom?"

"Okay." She trotted in the opposite direction.

My blood pressure hit a million over a million, and my headache wouldn't go away. Her temper appeared tamed for the moment, but I desperately needed to clean myself. Shame over my actions overwhelmed me, and I thought about confessing to Colisa. *Maybe if I just tell her the truth. She might understand if I tell her that I woke up after having sex with Antoinette, and I can't remember how it happened. Okay, maybe not.*

My wife returned to the kitchen with a confused expression. She carried a gray bottle with a white lid. "You plan on putting alcohol on burns? That doesn't sound like it goes together."

"Wow, you're right. Pain spazzed up for a second, but the worst is over. It's better already." I asked for the alcohol by reflex. "You can just set it on the counter. I'm gonna eat something and take a shower."

Colisa sat the bottle beside the sink and paused with her arms crossed. "This ain't the end of the world, Andre. But I have to be honest with you. I'm not feeling how things have been the last few weeks. You need to do something about it."

I blamed myself for the recent distance between us, and regretted whatever happened between Antoinette and me. "I will . . . I promise."

"Good night." She switched out the kitchen with her head up.

I exhaled a sigh of relief and placed my hand over my chest as it knocked out of control. My head pounded like I had a hangover from a night of heavy drinking. Fatigue sank in like never before, and I had no appetite. I stuck the food in the fridge and made my way to the couch. The sun came up through the living room window as I tried desperately to recall what led to me betraying my wife. Soon, I could no longer stay awake as everything went black.

My eyes popped open at 1:37 P.M. Confusion set in. I searched the house and found Colisa was already off to her route, and I assumed our baby girl was with her grandmother. It didn't take long to recall falling asleep on the couch after arguing with my wife.

Shit! I didn't call the job! I scrambled to the telephone and punched in the number to the service desk. No way did I want to have a no call, no show on my record after fifteen plus years of driving without a hiccup. The foreman answered and assured me Colisa had already called in on my behalf.

I finally got to the shower and washed the previous evening's events off me. Hunger crept up, so I went for the oxtail stew. As I sat the pot on the stove, the phone rang. The caller ID read: *Scott Investigations.*

Nerves shot down the center of my chest. I couldn't face Doug yet. Too many questions about what happened bothered me. I got my eat on and tried to piece the night together. Ten minutes later, the phone rang again. The caller ID read: *Antoinette Miller.*

She's got to give me some answers. I snatched the phone and put it to my ear. "What happened?"

"I'm sorry." She could've been a phone sex operator if she wanted. Her voice trickled through the receiver into my ear. "I don't know what got into me."

"What the hell, Antoinette?" The tone in my voice heightened. "Why can't I remember anything?"

"I dunno, Andre. All I know is that we crossed the line, and that shouldn't have happened." She paused for a moment. "It's all my fault. I seduced you. We can't let that happen again, and we can't let anyone know about it."

"Damn right! It's not gonna happen again." I paced the floor with my free hand against my forehead. "This is serious business. I'd be up shit's creek if my wife found out."

"Don't worry, nobody's gonna know." She spoke as if she tried to comfort me into thinking everything would be all right. "Doug walked right in on us, and he doesn't have a clue. It was a mistake. Let's just put it behind us."

I didn't feel as easy with it as she did, but I obviously had the most to lose.

After a few seconds of silence, she asked, "What time are you coming over today?"

"What? I'm not going to your place." Wrinkles formed in my forehead. "Are you crazy?"

"Wait! We have to figure out who killed my son," she said in a matter of fact tone. "You're still gonna help, right? The police aren't gonna do anything. You and Doug are good at this. Plus, you were there. I know you two can figure this out."

"Oh, no. I can't be a part of this." *This chick must be a Looney Tune. I can't be around her after what went down.* "My heart goes out, but I've got my own family to worry about."

Another moment of dead air passed between us. Antoinette's voice went up a couple notches. "Your family? Ah, yes. Maybe it's time I meet your wife."

What? That threw me for a loop. "Meet my wife? What you talking about, Antoinette?"

"I'm willing to keep what happened a secret. But if it's gonna stand in the way of you helping Doug, maybe I should rethink this." Her tone leveled out, and she spoke with confidence. "She still drives the bus, right? I can go up to the depot and introduce myself. Then we could discuss what her husband did last night."

"Bitch . . ." Anger almost took over, but I caught myself. I got a hold of my tone and spoke firmly. "Stay away from my wife and my family!"

"You think you can tell me what to do?" She giggled and hung up the phone. *Click!*

No she did not just hang up on me. Rage kicked in. I wanted to strangle Antoinette for threatening me. *Who the hell does she think she is?* I paced back and forward in the kitchen and debated with myself. My mind wondered about this chick meeting my wife outside of the job and ending my marriage. I scooped up the phone and called back the most recent number.

Antoinette answered on the second ring. "Did you have a change of heart? You gonna help Doug figure out what happened with my son?"

"I'm gonna help, but I don't want to hear you mention my wife ever again!" Bass came through in my voice as I made my point.

She laughed. "What happened is between me and you, Andre. Come on over."

"No! I'll help, but I'm not going to your house. I'll just get up with Doug. Don't call here again!"

Click!

I slammed the phone down and leaned against the counter with both hands. *How the hell did I get caught up in this Fatal Attraction shit?* I got my grub on and tended to my burns. After slipping on some jeans and a sweatshirt, I called Scott Investigations.

"I've been trying to call you," Doug said. "Your cell phone is going straight to voicemail."

"Yeah, I lost it," I replied. "I'm sure the battery is shot by now. What's the dealio?"

"This is the day your boy with the Bears coat rides the Number Nine." Doug reminded me of the witness that may have gotten a good look at the shooter. "I'm gonna stake out 71st and Ashland and see if I can get some information from the young man. You comin'?"

Goosebumps popped up on my arms. Through all the commotion of betraying my wife, I still got excited about finding the link that would solve this case. "Yeah, I'm comin'."

Doug's smile shined through in his voice. "Good. Meet me at Antoinette's and we'll go over the—"

"No. I'm not meeting you at her house," I said, interrupting him in mid-sentence. "I'll meet you at the Hip-Hop Mickey D's right off the Dan Ryan."

Soon as Doug and I ended the call, I reeled around and cast my eyes upon my nephew. He caught me off guard a little. "Dorian?"

"It's me in the flesh, Uncle Dre." He inhaled deeply and stuck out his chest. "Sounds like you're about to go. Can I roll?"

"Not this time, son." I grabbed my keys off the counter. "This may be a little too dangerous for youngstas."

He sucked his teeth and pouted, leaving out the room.

I bundled up in layers and warmed up the truck. Doug met me in the McDonald's parking lot where he revealed he got information about the singer that took the stage before us. He knew exactly where to find her that afternoon. But first, we hit the bus stop where the witness usually got off on my route. The heat gushed out the vents in the Ford Escort as we arrived at our spot. Two buses passed by without stopping before a bus pulled over and opened its door.

A young man stepped off wearing a Bears coat and a backpack. The bus pulled away as he waited for the light to cross the street.

Doug sat up in his seat and pointed with excitement. "There's our guy! Let's get him!"

Chapter Ten:
House Party

I squinted and stared in the direction of the person at the bus stop. Doug disabled the ignition and opened his door. I zeroed in on the man's face.

"Wait!" I got a load of dude as he glanced back and forward to check traffic. "That's not him."

"It's not him?" Confusion came over Doug. "But he's wearing a Bears coat."

"Damn right he's wearing a Bears coat." I stared at him to make sure as he crossed the street. "But that's not our man. He's not that tall, and he doesn't have braids."

Doug shut the door and returned the key to the ignition. "Reach in the glove compartment and grab those binoculars. You let me know when you see 'im."

"My bus will be coming along here shortly." I unfolded the binoculars and noticed two mini tablets, two fancy cell phones, and several small chips. "What are these chip things?"

He peeked at the glove compartment and then returned his attention to his surroundings. "Memory cards. That's where I save any pictures, videos, or audio recordings."

"Everything is all digital now." I closed the glove compartment and observed three groups of college students crossing the street. "So why aren't you a cop anymore? I mean, I liked being a part of campus security back in the day, but it meant everything to you. You always wanted to be five-O. What happened?"

"A lot." Doug made eye contact with me. "Let's just say it was hard to do my job and stay within the rules. I'll leave it at that."

"I ain't mad at ya'." I wondered how I could lead the conversation to Antoinette when I wasn't supposed to be aware of him wanting to get back with her. "So you ain't got no woman at home, man? You haven't said anything about a Mrs. Scott."

"I haven't had a lot of luck in that department." The expression on his face never changed. "I spend a lotta time trying to catch the bad guy and not enough time on the home front. But who knows? Maybe Miss Right is still out there."

Maybe, but it sure as hell ain't Antoinette. My attention hit the next bus approaching. "This is the one I would be driving today. This is my bus."

We sat up in our seats and focused on the people getting off. The binoculars gave me a close up view of everyone's face. Six people got off the bus and none of them matched the witness's description.

"He's not on this one either." I removed the binoculars from my eyes. "He definitely comes this way on a regular basis. I say we hang in here for a few more buses to see if he shows."

"Sounds like a plan. I haven't been on a stakeout with a partner since I left the force." Doug let his seat back. "My old partner is a good cop. Last night, he let me know they don't think this was done by the GDs. They think the Vice Lords did it."

"But that doesn't make any sense." I frowned with confusion. "MC ET was a straight up Vice Lord himself. Why would they take out one of their own?"

"That's a good question." Doug scanned the area from right to left before checking the rearview mirror. "And I hope this kid can ID a suspect, so we can shed some light on the situation."

"I hear you." I checked the road for the next bus. "This private eye situation is sweet. You gotta be the luckiest man in the world."

"What are you talking about?" Doug raised one eyebrow and looked at me like I was crazy. "You're the lucky one. You got the big house, the family, damn near twenty years vested on the job. Some of us ain't got it like that."

"You're right about that, home boy. I am pretty lucky." I knew Colisa was a good catch when I married her. She proves me right time and time again. "You'll never hear me say I was dealt a bad hand."

Doug rubbed his chin. "I might try to see what Antoinette is talking about once all this is over."

There, he brought it up. No way could I let my boy get caught up. "I'm not too sure about that, fam'. She doesn't seem like the same girl we knew a long time ago."

"Well, none of us are the same people." Doug scanned the area from left to right.

"Damn right." I grabbed the binoculars with one hand and pointed out the window with the other. "Another bus is coming."

This one pulled up and let out seven people as it picked up three. Our witness wasn't on that one either. Doug and I waited for the next four buses. The young man in the Bears coat and the headphones never showed up. Time expired for us on that stakeout because we had to follow a different lead. The singer that took the stage before us was scheduled to be interviewed on WKKC. They broadcast from Kennedy-King College located right up the way from us. We headed west on 71st Street and parked across the avenue from one of the City Colleges of Chicago.

Doug led the way through the halls of the school. We took the elevator up several flights and entered the offices of the radio station. The security guard eyeballed Doug and gave him an upward head nod. Doug returned the gesture, and we waltzed right past. We came to a window and got a clear view of the broadcast studio. The artist that went on before us at the show sat at a microphone at one end of a table. Two DJs leaned into mics on the other side. We couldn't hear them through the glass. However, their voices flowed amplified from speakers embedded in the ceiling above us.

"This is Shavonn and Vanzant on the afternoon drive, and we've been kickin' it with Kee-Kee Rose!" The female DJ had dimples and rocked a blonde streak from the top of a frizzy afro. *"Thank you for comin' through!"*

Kee-Kee Rose leaned into the mic as she held one hand on her headphones. *"Oh, thank you for having me. The pleasure is all mine."*

The male DJ wore a green shirt and sported waves with a fresh line up. *"You gonna come back again and see us soon?"*

"Of course I will. Anytime you'll have me," Kee-Kee Rose replied.

Music came out of nowhere as the female DJ spoke over it. *"We're gonna leave you with Kee-Kee's hit single, 'Please Stay!' We'll see you next time on WKKC!"*

The vocals of the song dropped in like clockwork. All three of them took off their headphones as they smiled and shook hands. Their lips moved, but we could no longer hear their voices.

"Perfect timing." Doug crossed his arms as he glanced at me. "I think it's time we see if we can get Miss Rose to give us something she doesn't even know she knows."

Doug and I chilled at a door outside the broadcast room as she stepped out with Shavonn and Vanzant. They went one way, while Kee-Kee locked in on me and maintained eye contact as she approached.

"I remember those eyes. You were at the concert the other night." Her hair went down her back, and she made a gray turtleneck type of shirt look good. "Do they know who did this yet?"

"No, but that's what we wanna talk to you about. I'm Andre, and this is my boy, Doug." I pointed to him with my thumb as I relaxed my voice to a mellow pitch. "He's investigating the shooting on behalf of MC ET's mother. We're wondering if we could ask a few questions."

"Of course. Anything I can do to help," she resounded with eagerness. "But I've already told the police everything I know."

Doug spoke in a friendly tone. "You mind telling *us* what happened?"

"No, not at all. I finished my set, left the stage, and passed right by you guys." She glanced at me as she pointed my way. Her eyes moved to Doug. "I got back stage, and the bouncers cleared the area. When I arrived at the dressing room, I glanced around. The space was clear, except for the janitor. I was already in the room when I heard the gunshots."

The janitor? I struggled to remember a janitor on the scene.

Doug and I soaked it in as he asked, "What did you do next?"

"I fell to the floor and covered my head." Her eyebrows went up as she put her hands above her hair. "I stayed in the room until one of the bouncers came in to check."

"Did you see anything that may have been suspicious?" Doug stuck his hand out in front of himself. "Anything or anyone that may have looked out of place?"

"Well, maybe . . ." She paused and put her finger on her chin. Her eyes rolled upward as her wheels turned. She shook her head no. "Nah, never mind."

I raised one eyebrow. "What?"

"Well, I didn't say anything about this before, and I won't acknowledge saying it right now." She hesitated, as if awaiting our approval.

"As far as I'm concerned, this conversation never happened," Doug replied.

"I didn't see the shooting, but I saw the janitor." Her lips twisted. "I understand he told the police he didn't see anything. But he was right there when I closed the door to my room. Seems like he should've had a perfect view."

Oh yeah, the janitor! She sparked the memory of the dark skinned, green-eyed man in his sixties. My father worked as a detective for the Chicago Police Department. He disappeared in the line of duty during my teenage years. CPD presumed him dead. The janitor reminded me of him.

"Interesting. That's a good piece of news to investigate." Doug reached in his pocket and pulled out his card. "Here's my number. Can we keep in touch?"

Kee-Kee Rose agreed and exchanged information with Doug. She exited down the hall as Doug and I spoke among ourselves.

"So the janitor could be hiding something. Maybe we should check him out." I recalled seeing old boy talk to police that night.

"That might be a plan," Doug agreed. "But I'd rather find your boy in the Bears jacket. We know for a fact he got a good look at whoever you chased in the alley."

We headed to the elevator.

"Wait!" I froze in my tracks as I saw the female DJ getting in the elevator at the very end of the hallway. The door closed as she spoke with a young man wearing a Bears coat with headphones around his neck. "That's him! Hold that elevator!"

Doug and I took off sprinting through the hall. She caught view of us and appeared to reach to touch the button to keep the door open, but it was too late. We approached the elevator, and the door shut tight in front of us. Doug and I glanced around and found the sign that led to the stairs. He bolted through the door first as I followed. Leaping several stairs at a time, we descended nine flights. We hit the first floor and shot through another door before heading to the elevator.

It opened and several other people got off. *Where'd they go?* I huffed and puffed as Doug and I scanned the area.

"Look," Doug said as he grabbed my arm with one hand and pointed with the other. "There's the DJ!"

Shavonn chilled near the front desk, speaking with an older woman. We strolled quickly to get to her side.

"Hey, sorry I couldn't stop the elevator." Shavonn smiled as she apologized.

Doug's eyebrows came together as he spoke. "Where's the guy you were just with?"

"Who? Simone?" She gave us a confused look for a split second. "He just walked outside."

We trotted through the door. The cold wind met me in the face as the sun set. Doug and I glanced around the yard three hundred sixty degrees, but the man in the Bears jacket was nowhere to be found. *Damn it!*

We stepped in the building and approached the DJ.

"Who was that?" Doug tried to catch his breath as he spoke.

"That's our sound engineer, Simone," the young lady said. "Is everything okay?"

"Yes, it's fine," I said. We couldn't afford to come off too hard, because we needed her cooperation. "He's exactly who we came to see. You guys sound nice on the radio."

"Thank you," she replied with a smile that lit up the area.

"We might be able to use Simone's skills. He's good, and we might have a gig for him." Once I noticed her eyes light up, I hit her with the question that mattered. "Where can we find him?"

"Oh, he would love that! He'll be back tomorrow." She paused for a second and a half as she glanced in the cut. "Or I'm sure he'll be at the party. It's one of the Ques birthday today. Everybody's gonna be on 56th and Halsted if you want to go. I recommend showing up early."

The clock struck 5:30 P.M. and darkness surrounded us. The Escort got us through rush hour traffic and to the block of the

Que party. Dozens of young adults flocked into a residential two-flat. The heat beat me in the face as we scoped out the place for two hours. Different color strobe lights flashed through the front window on the second floor as more people piled into the building. At 9:19 P.M., Simone strolled down the street.

"There's our man!" I gave a head nod in the direction of the witness. "You want to follow him in, or wait 'til he comes out?"

"Don't want to lose him." Doug turned off the ignition. "That's the third Bears coat we've seen while sitting here. Let's keep him within sight."

We jogged across the street and followed the crowd into the house party. The witness made his way in the main entrance on the side of the crib. Four other people entered before Doug and me. Muffled music thumped the walls as eight people lamped right inside the entrance. The aroma of premium weed hit me in the nose as the door shut behind me. I said excuse me several times as we went up the stairs. People crowded each other side by side in the area at the top. Moving through the crowd became a lot more difficult.

Inside the apartment, bodies packed in like sardines in a can. Speakers on stands on the opposite side of a huge living room blasted music loud and clear. At least fifty people filled every visible space in the house. Two strobe lights and two beacons lit up the darkness with a rainbow of colors. "Adorn" by Miguel banged through the air.

Doug grabbed my arm and nodded to the left. Simone smiled at a young lady as their bodies mashed against each other, and everyone else's surrounding them. We attempted the slow process of moving through the crowd. Doug and I slithered through people as more bodies piled in the door behind us. I unzipped my coat as sweat rolled down my neck. Several long moments later, we reached the witness.

I leaned into his ear and shouted over the music. "Let me holla at you for a minute!"

He twisted around. His eyebrows went up and gave me the impression that he recognized me. He yelled over the music. "What's up!"

"We wanna talk to you about what happened at the concert the other night!" I filled him in on the nature of the conversation.

Simone's eyes went back and forward between Doug and me, and then he stared past us. I rotated my head and caught two men in nighttime shades possibly watching us.

"Naw, man! I don't know what y'all talkin' 'bout! Excuse me!" Simone tried to get by us, but it was too crowded to move.

"It will just take a couple minutes, little brotha!" I had to get something from him while I had the chance. He was our best hope. "We won't take too much of your time!"

"Look, man! I know what you want, and I ain't see nuthin'!" He squirmed and shuffled, but we all jammed together shoulder to shoulder. "Just leave me alone!"

"Shot Caller" by French Montana mixed in on cue.

The crowd went wild. The ladies screamed "Hey" and the fellas yelled "Ho!" Everyone collectively bounced up and down to the beat. All of our weight hit the bottom of the room at the same time, and the floor creaked as it bounced up and down like a trampoline.

"WHOA!" the crowd bellowed all together. Everyone relaxed with the bouncing. The floor leveled out and stopped moving.

"I didn't like how that felt!" Doug leaned into my shoulder. "Let's get outta here!"

"Hold up!" I yelled over the music at Doug, and then directed my attention to Simone. "Just meet us outside, and it will be over just like that! You know me from the bus, man!"

He stared past me again. I peeped out the corner of my eye and saw the same two men.

"Just beat it, man!" He frowned up and pleaded for me to leave him alone. "Can't you take a hint?"

"Is it because of those two clowns over there with the shades on?" I pointed in their direction with my thumb.

"Man, just get away from me!" Simone desperately tried to move through the crowd, but too many people packed the house.

"Atomic Dog" by George Clinton slammed in right on time.

Virtually everyone snapped and gave an outcry of pleasure. The Que-dogs barked to the top of their lungs as the crowd stomped to the beat. Other fraternities shouted their chants, each trying to be louder than the other. The floor sprung up and descended more aggressively as people jammed to the music with approval.

The floor creaked loud as hell on each down beat.

"Whoa!" everyone yelled as we collectively realized that wasn't right.

CRACK!

The beam supporting one side of the floor gave way. The congregation of people tumbled in one direction.

I frowned with disbelief as I grabbed the two closest people to my hands. My jacket tugged in several directions as others near me reacted the same way. From my side of the room, the floor tilted to the left.

CRACK!

Another beam popped. The slope in the floor grew steeper.

I yelled out my objection, "No!"

It ended up being one of many cries as the party screamed in terror. My feet slid from up under me as people rammed into my lower body. I tumbled to the floor along with the surrounding crowd and landed on at least three bodies while others piled on me. The music stopped.

The foundation gave three more creaks and a final crack. The center of the landing collapsed from wall to wall.

My eyes popped wide open as I slid across the ground to the

rupture in the floor along with dozens of partygoers. I crashed into several bodies as we met in the middle. Someone's foot kicked me in the face. Everyone descended through the opening in the floor to the apartment below.

Chapter Eleven:
Simone

Body by body, we dropped to the first floor. I landed on two people and felt the impact of at least three others that slammed down on me.

Pain shot through my body from head to toe. I felt a little mixed up as I pushed people off and away. Screams rang out into the night. Dust, debris, and pieces of wood and plaster crashed on top of the pile. Several chairs and the speakers from the second floor joined the bodies on the first floor. Someone stepped on my palm as they tried to get up.

"AHHH!" I yanked my hand back and coughed a few times. Dust got onto my clothes, my hair, and up my nose. I wiped my face and scanned the area. Simone came to his knees coughing up a storm. *Where's Doug?*

Some of the crowd stumbled right up and dusted themselves off. One guy yelled to the top of his lungs in pain as he used one hand to hold the opposite arm close to his body. Three people immediately limped to attend to a girl who grabbed her ribs as her body draped across the floor.

My shoulder throbbed as I rose to one knee. I coughed a few

more times and eventually caught my breath.

A girl screamed as she discovered her friend. "She's not moving!"

I came to my feet and approached the girl lying there. Her friend went hysterical as a muscle bound dude covered in dust checked her pulse. He shook his head no, and she screamed.

I closed my eyes and turned away. *Where the heck is Doug?* Again I scanned the area and caught Simone leaning his hands against the wall as he caught his breath.

"You all right?" I asked.

"My ankle is jacked up." He coughed a few more times and kept the weight off his foot. "It hurts when I stand on it."

"Lemme help you over to one of these chairs, man." I positioned myself as he leaned on me. We took three steps together. "Don't put too much pressure on it."

"Wait. I think I can walk on it." He let me go and limped past several people to a dining room chair. "I'm good. I'll be all right."

Someone opened the door to the apartment, and several people rushed in from upstairs. They scrambled around to help the injured partygoers. At least three people appeared to be on the phone with 911 trying to get help. Soon, I caught Doug trying to help make a girl comfortable against the wall. She favored her right leg and arm as she cried.

I dusted myself off as I approached him. "Doug! You all right?"

"Yeah, I came out okay." He stood up as the young lady's friends consoled her. "This girl's arm is broken. Somebody call for help."

"It's about a billion people on the phone with Emergency Services right now." I surveyed the apartment and soaked in the pandemonium. "How in the hell did this happen?"

"I don't know, man. It's crazy!" Doug moved to take a closer look at the wreckage. The ceiling remained attached to the foundation around the top of the walls. However, it sunk in and parted down the middle like Moses was upstairs, and the living room above was the Red Sea. Doug pointed to the damage. "Look at this!"

The apartment had a nice paint job. However, the wooden beams in between the surface were mostly black.

I stood beside him and glanced up. "That can't be right. Is it supposed to be like that?"

"No. This building has been on fire before." Doug shook his head as he grimaced. "Whoever half-repaired this should have their ass kicked. The building is not fit to live in."

We did our best to help the injured as everyone waited for help to arrive. The two men with nighttime shades stood in front of Simone as he leaned against the wall to support himself. They frowned and pointed their fingers in his face. Simone wore a threatened expression.

I nudged Doug to get his attention. "Check this out."

We got a load of the thugs aggressive gestures. Doug and I made eye contact. Then we stormed in Simone's direction.

"Is there a problem here?" I positioned myself to one side of the thugs as Doug surrounded them on the other.

The one nearest to me wore a red coat. He tilted his head as he stared at me. "I think you need to step away from me, old man."

Did this muthafucka just call me old man? I frowned and beamed a hole in his pupils with my eyes.

Doug jumped in as he pointed at Simone with his thumb. "This young man is hurt. We need to get him some medical attention."

"Naw, man. I'm fine." Simone held both his palms out as he tried to move around me. "I'm straight, y'all. I can make it alone. If everyone will just excuse me."

The one in the red snatched Simone by his coat using both hands. He wore a baseball cap to the back in the wintertime.

"Where the fuck do you think you're going?"

Simone tugged to get away.

"Hey!" My arm chopped across the thug's forearm and sliced Simone from his grip. I hopped between them and faced the man in the red coat. "All that ain't even necessary!"

"Are you crazy?" The thug in red came up and nudged me with both his palms in my shoulders. "You tryna get dropped?"

I braced myself and thrust all my strength into shoving him in his chest.

He stumbled backward and crashed to the floor. Two people trying to get through the crowd tripped over him and toppled to the carpet. Doug jumped in front of me and reached behind himself for his gun. The thug came to his feet as he opened his coat. He reached for a pistol handle sticking up above the rim of his pants.

His partner wore a black coat with a red scarf. He hopped in the middle of the ruckus as he grabbed his boy's wrists. "No! Don't pull that out in here! Five-O is already on the way!"

The dude in the red coat stopped struggling to get past his boy. He gazed at us with anger. "This ain't over. You hear me! I'm gone kill you!"

Police sirens faded up from the distance.

"Hold that down, people!" His boy shoved him toward the back door.

He gave in and shuffled away without taking his eyes off us. Doug and I stood our ground as we remained squared off in his direction. As soon as they made their way out the door, we swiveled around to face Simone. We got a view of his backside as he limped away toward the front door.

"Hey, wait a minute!" I yelled for his attention as Doug and I made our way through the commotion. "Let us help you. Wait!"

Simone ignored us and hobbled out the front door. Frigid air swooped in as we tailed him. We caught up with him as he hit the sidewalk.

"Slow down, lil' brotha'." I got at him with a friendly tone to try to gain his trust.

Doug hit him with the voice of logic. "Let us help you. You might want to have somebody look at your ankle."

"Look, why don't y'all just leave me alone!" He staggered away from us with a frown on his face. "You've caused enough trouble already. Beat it!"

We stood there in the cold as he waddled away. Several people helped the girl out of the house who cried over her friend. Others scattered in every direction. The first cop car pulled up to the scene.

"Let's get outta here." Doug led the way to the car.

"That was a jacked up turn of events." I shut the door behind me as I got in the ride. "And we didn't even get anything out of our witness."

"No kidding." Doug started the vehicle and shifted into gear. "We're not giving up on this guy right now. He's our best hope. We know he saw the murderer's face."

"Those other cats are Vice Lords." The heat hit me in the face as we rolled through the block, trying not to run anyone over. We busted a left at the corner. "I wonder what kind of business they have with Simone. They can't be sweatin' him about this case. Can they?"

"I plan on asking him that soon, but I wouldn't think so." Doug scoped out the area ahead of us. "Hey, we might just get the chance to ask him sooner than I expected. Look!"

I followed Doug's eyes and caught Simone limping into a building up the block. We parked the ride across the street and huffed it to the other side. The sign above the door read: *Robert Edward's.* Doug hit the doorbell, and we got buzzed into a pool hall. The door shut behind us. Eight pool tables lined up from wall to wall with a game going on each one. Most of the people stopped in their tracks to glance our way. Simone sat in a small lounge area near the front of a counter with a cash register on it. We strolled up on him as he leaned back in his chair.

He could really be hurt. I didn't want to bombard him with questions about the murder right away. "Are you okay, lil' brotha?"

"I'm good, man. My ankle is just a little sore." He raised his leg and rested it on the chair beside him. "Look, I know y'all have good intentions. But just leave me alone, and this will all go away."

"What will all go away?" Doug asked.

Simone glanced over his shoulders as if to make sure nobody listened in. He made eye contact with me as he whispered, "Somebody saw me point you in the direction of the shooter the other night. The next day, they threatened to kill me if I said anything else. Those two goons have been watching me ever since."

"Don't listen to them. We need you to help us out and do the right thing, man." Doug stood over him and spoke with a strong voice. "We know the shooter ran right past you."

"Don't you understand? I can't help you." His voice got louder. "Just leave me alone! I didn't see or hear anything. In fact, I wasn't even there!"

"Is everything okay over here?" A bald, dark skinned man in his late fifties approached us. "You gentlemen look like you're having a rough night."

"Everything is under control." Doug faced the man and flashed his badge quickly. He returned it to his pocket. "Just conducting an investigation."

"No problem, officer." The man's voice rang deep. "Anything I can do to help, but you're scaring my customers."

"Just give us a minute." Doug approached the man. He spoke in his ear as he led him away.

"Dude is five-O?" Simone's eyes bucked open. "Man, I can't be talkin' to y'all."

I squatted to his level as I whispered loud enough for him to hear. "Hold it down, homie. My boy is just frontin' to keep old boy off us. Meanwhile, we're gonna have to get outta here soon. But we need you to help us first. You know me, man. Right?"

"Yeah, I know you. You drive the Number Nine during the afternoon." Simone frowned as he looked me up and down. "And you rapped with Inner City Youth back in the day."

My head jerked back in shock. He should've known me from the bus, but I had no clue he knew of me otherwise.

He must have recognized the confusion on my face as he explained, "My older brother used to play y'all song on cassette."

"Good. So you know I ain't on no bs." I needed him to trust me, and I had nothing to lose by telling him the truth. "My boy is a private investigator. MC ET's mother hired him to find out who did this to her son. We just need your help right quick, lil' brotha. You don't have to testify or ever see us again."

"I don't know, man." Simone shook his head back and forward. "The Vice Lords ain't no joke."

"Just trust me. You'll be doing the right thing." I realized this was as close as I'd come to getting something out of him. So I went for it. "It ain't right if Stallion Pee did this and gets away with it."

Simone took a deep breath and rolled his eyes at me. He glanced over his shoulders. "It wasn't Stallion Pee."

Surprise overcame me. I got caught up in the spin the media put on the rivalry between the two artists. My mind made him a primary suspect. "So who was it . . . who killed those people?"

"I don't know."

What the . . . Is this kid fucking with me? I came to a full stand and gazed down on him. "What do you mean, you don't know?"

"I don't know his name." Simone held his head up and sat straight. "But I know it wasn't Stallion Pee."

I raised one eyebrow and grabbed my chin. "Do you think

you'll recognize him if you see his face?"

"Naw, man. You said no testifying, and I wouldn't have to see y'all again." Simone shook his head. "Just get away and get outta here before y'all get me killed!"

"Wait, hold on." I was losing him. My wheels rotated as I tried to get him back. "You don't have to do anything you don't want to do."

Doug strolled in our direction. "What's going on?"

"He doesn't know the killer's name, but he might recognize his face." I caught Doug up to speed. "Can he help us?"

Doug directed his attention to Simone. "Can we get you to come to the car and look at some pictures? I'll pull them up on my tablet and nobody else will know. We'll drop you off anywhere you want after that."

Simone exhaled as his eyes rolled to the sky. He twisted his lips as he debated with himself. "If I do this, y'all gone leave me alone?"

"Trust us. We'll never bother you again." Doug moved beside Simone and squatted as he reached to assist him up. "C'mon, we'll help you to the car."

Simone grabbed onto Doug's arm and dragged himself to a stand. They took a few steps together, before Simone pulled away and staggered along on his own. I followed them to the front door and out into the cold night. The wind roared through us as we stepped to the curb. I scanned the street from right to left, and we waited for a break in traffic. A gap arrived, so we strolled into the street. Doug and Simone followed behind me as Doug assisted him as much as he would allow. I stepped around to the passenger side of the ride.

A burgundy Chevy shot out of a parking spot about fifty yards behind us with no headlights on. It raced in our direction and steered to the other side of Doug and Simone. The car slowed to a stop. Down came the back passenger side window. An automatic weapon stuck out clenched by two hands wearing black gloves. A black male wearing a red bandana around his face, a black skullcap, and shades gripped the trigger.

My heart skipped a beat. *Oh shit!* I yelled to get Doug and Simone's attention. "Drive-by!"

The triggerman aimed in our direction and unloaded.

Rat-tat-tat-tat-tat-tat!

Chapter Twelve:
Witness Down

I dived face-first to the concrete, closed my eyes, and covered the back of my head with both hands. *Rat-tat-tat-tat-tat-tat!* The weapon rattled off multiple shots as the windows of the ride shattered and bullets ricocheted in every direction.

Doug and Simone's voices both echoed cries into the night.

The tires of the burgundy car burned rubber as the car sped away.

SCREECH!

I opened my eyes, peeped under the car, and caught a view of Doug and Simone. Their bodies shook with convulsions. Doug's torso lay on top of Simone's.

"No!" I came to my feet and scrambled around the car.

The burgundy car accelerated up the avenue at top speed. Brake lights came on, and the tires squealed as it avoided traffic at the intersection.

Doug rolled off Simone. Blood covered them both. Doug grabbed onto a bullet wound in his upper chest near his left shoulder. Blood gushed out the front and rear. Simone rested on his back with his hands extended to either side as his body gyrated along the ground. He faced the sky while blood flushed from four bullets to the chest. Doug yelled out once in pain, and then huffed and puffed like he'd just run a marathon.

Goddamn it, no! I rushed to Simone's side, fell to the ground, and lifted the back of his head with both hands like a newborn baby. He snatched and swiped at thin air as his eyes bulged from his head.

"Damn, man! I'm sorry!" Guilt sank in. I cuffed my forearm and rested the back of his head against my bicep. "Hang on, lil' brotha! Hang on!"

The old man stormed out the pool hall with at least a dozen of his customers at his back. "What happened?"

I glanced at them and screamed, "Get some fucking help!"

The old man pointed at someone as he nodded at two other people. The one guy hopped on the cell right away, and the others rushed to help Doug.

Veins popped out of Simone's forehead. His mouth opened and closed, but no air moved in or out.

This is not happening! I raised his head and grabbed his cheeks. "Hang in there, fam'! Breathe! Breathe!"

Blood flushed from Simone's mouth and rolled over my hand. His forehead wrinkled, and his eyes grew glossy as he strained to take a breath.

I slapped his cheek and jiggled his face around. "C'mon, lil' brotha! Fight!"

More blood poured from his mouth and clotted with saliva between his teeth. His eyeballs forced their way to the back of his head. Blood from his chest and back covered the front of my coat and most of my jeans. I held him as we posed in a puddle of blood. He stopped moving.

A chill came over me as I glanced up the street at the burgundy car stalled at the streetlight. The driver choked the ignition. It turned over and over, but it wouldn't start. I rested Simone's head on an ice patch drenched in blood before checking on Doug. They removed his bad arm from his coat. A light-skinned man in a brown hat mashed a white rag against the front of Doug's shoulder. Most of the towel turned red as blood seeped around the edges. A lady in a pink scarf and furry hood pressed a rag against his back.

"We're trying to get him to stop bleeding," the man said as he came off like a doctor.

I made eye contact with Doug. "Are you all right?"

"My fingers are numb." He struggled to talk and catch his breath. "It's cold."

VROOM!

The shooter's car started, and the driver fired up the engine like a race car.

My hands shot out in front of me. "They're gonna get away!"

Doug's eyes stayed connected with mine. He grabbed his keys out his pocket with his good hand and tossed them to me. "This is all you!"

The keys dropped out the sky and into my blood covered palms. I glanced around at the people from the pool hall.

SCREECH!

The shooter's ride took off through a red light. The burgundy car forged ahead at a rate of acceleration too fast for a residential area.

I sprung into the driver side of the Escort, ignited the ignition, and snatched it into gear. The tires burned rubber as I strapped on my seat belt and steered around Simone's body. Cold air shot in through the back driver side window as I zoomed up the block. Glass crunched up under my ass. I adjusted the seat. My foot rammed the accelerator, and I flew through the red light.

The shooter's vehicle zipped up the road for two blocks. Brake lights came on, and they skidded into a right turn.

My speed picked up as I kept an eye out for pedestrians. I bolted down a clear street with only three parked cars. This car had an Escort body, but it rolled like it had eight cylinders under the hood. I hit the right turn and forgot about the road conditions. The rear of the car slid ahead of me. I ripped the steering wheel to the left and skidded an additional ten feet before the front of the car caught up and edged ahead. My hands took the wheel to the right and I guided the ride back on track.

The getaway car stayed ahead of me on the same street for five blocks. It flashed a left turn signal as they obeyed a red light.

"Achoo!" I sneezed as I closed in on the Chevy. The heat blasted through the vents, but cold air rushed in the window to the back of my head. I pulled up behind their car and put the Escort in park. Three men moved around in the ride ahead of me.

My seat belt came off , and I climbed in the rear of the Escort to let the backseat forward. I grabbed the sawed off shotgun from the wall of the trunk and placed it in the front seat. The seat belt snapped into place as the green arrow signaled the turning lane to proceed.

They pulled off and casually made a left. I remained a half car length behind them as they rolled another three blocks. They made a right, and I followed. Everyone in the car turned and gazed my way as they realized I tailed them.

SCREECH!

The driver punched it, and they sped off at top speed. I frowned as I gave it some gas and tried to keep pace. My hand gripped the steering wheel at twelve o'clock as I guided the ride down the boulevard. The Chevy hooked a hard left and jetted down another block with a full head of steam.

My momentum picked up as I advanced down the road and whirled into the left lane. The throttle opened up and I propelled the Escort like a Mustang. I flew up the street and closed in on them with the quickness.

Their brake lights came on, and the burgundy Chevy slowed all of a sudden. The car rolled a few additional feet and angled slightly before it came to an abrupt stop.

Oh shit! I slammed on the brakes. The wheels of the Escort shrieked. Rubber burned as I screeched in their direction. My elbows locked as I grabbed the steering wheel with both hands. The car glided along the pavement and walloped into the rear left corner of the Chevy.

WHAM!

The rear of Doug's car lifted off the ground. My body shot forward. The seat belt tightened like a noose and snapped me out of thin air. The back wheels landed, and I bounced with the car as the seat belt clung me to the driver seat.

The Chevy skidded forward about thirty yards while doing a one-eighty. It came to a stop facing me and wobbled in place.

Pain punched my shoulder. I grabbed at it and shook my head from left to right.

The passenger in the other car pointed at me with aggression. *Brown-skinned black male. Can't make out his face.* The driver revved the engine.

SCREECH!

He blazed the road like a Pro Stock drag racer and accelerated in my direction.

What the fuck! My eyes bucked, and I froze like a deer caught in headlights . "No!"

The car raced at me without slowing down. It thwacked into the front left side of the Escort.

CRASH!

My head bounced around, and my arms shot out to the sides. Both cars slid along the street. The right side of Doug's car mashed into a parked truck. My chest thumped as I got a load of the situation. The Chevy and the truck sandwiched me in. The Ford Escort shut off.

The driver put the car in reverse, rolled backward about twenty yards, and came to a stop. The car jerked as he shifted into drive. Tires burned rubber, and they darted in my direction.

No! I spun the key forward in the ignition. The engine turned over and over, but didn't ignite.

WHAM!

They rammed into the same area of Doug's car.

My bell rung. Pressure impacted my entire body. I swayed back and forward as much as the seat belt would allow. Bright stars blurred my vision as I tried to focus in on the other car.

They rolled backward with a substantial amount of damage. The burgundy Chevy busted a three-point turn and scooted up the way.

Wow! Disbelief hit me like a mug. I placed my palms on either side of my face and blinked hard four times. My head wobbled side to side to get the cobwebs out. Five seconds later, I got angry.

The engine turned over. I tried to start the ride, but I had no luck. *I'm in drive.* I shifted the gear to neutral. It cranked for two seconds and ignited.

VROOM!

I placed my foot on the gas, and then yanked it into drive. The tires screeched as the rear of Doug's car scraped against the truck on the other side of me. I pulled off in the same direction as the thugs. The banged up ride got a move on up the street for ten seconds before arriving at a downward slope. The car sped up as I rolled down a hill. I stepped on the brake, and the pedal gave all the way to the floor.

What the fuck! My foot came up and stomped down three times on a brake that went soft. "No, not this!"

Doug's car picked up speed. My elbows locked again, and I steered with a tight grip at ten and two o'clock. I zipped down the hill and approached a red light. A Mac truck advanced toward the intersection from the left. A CTA bus drew near on the right.

My eyelids went all the way up. I maintained a straight path and zoomed into the junction.

The bus and the truck crossed paths and rolled off in opposite directions. The vehicles parted ways *just* in enough time to create room for me to coast through the red light.

I kept the brake to the floor, but the car accelerated down the hill into an open lot. The car rambled through four construction horses and closed in on a five-foot mountain of dirt. I ripped the steering wheel to the right. The two left tires rolled up the heap. They went over and cleared the other side of the pile. The left side of Doug's car sailed in midair as the right side rolled forward on two wheels. The passenger side door hit the concrete, and the car skidded forward. The Escort tipped over the rest of the way and landed on its roof. The metal scraped the ground as the top of the car glided along the pavement.

I hung upside down. The seat belt suspended me in midair. My life flashed before my eyes as the car slid along the concrete wrong side up.

Sparks shot out in every direction. I glided along until the back of the car hit a fire hydrant. The front moved forward as the rear rolled off the fireplug, causing the ride to revolve three hundred and sixty degrees.

The car skidded along on the roof, rotating several times until it rammed into a solid structure.

WHAM!

Chapter Thirteen:
Trapped

*H*OOOOOONK!

The horn blared one long continuous shriek.

"I can't get either door open!" A man's voice faded in from nowhere. "You! Try the other side!"

"Sir! Are you okay?" A faint female voice in the distance got my attention. "Can you hear me? If you can hear me, move your fingers."

"He's not moving!" the man shouted over the noise. "Go get some help!"

"Hell naw!" A younger male voice came from a distance. "That nigga's car flipped over!"

"Oh my God! He's dead!" A different lady gave her opinion. "What happened?"

"I saw it!" Another young male's voice checked in. "He lost control coming down the hill and just missed a bus and a truck. The car flipped over that dirt pile."

The blaring racket annoyed me to death. Gravity shot to my

crown, and I grew more baffled by the second. *Where am I?*

"Move him off the horn," the man suggested.

"No! Don't touch him!" the first lady advised. "Wait until help arrives."

"Hurry up and call somebody!" another random voice weighed in. "I saw the crash, too. Unbelievable!"

"These doors won't come open, either!" the younger voice said.

My head throbbed, and a tremendous amount of pressure got my attention. All of a sudden, the sensation of gargling took over. My mouth filled with liquid and some of it went down the wrong pipe. I coughed up a frenzy.

"He's moving!" The original lady's voice escalated with excitement.

The horn stopped as I hacked it up big time. My eyes popped open, and my arms bumped against random objects. Pressure rushed to my dome in a strange way. Everything blurred, and I felt confined in a small space.

"Try to stay calm. It's gonna be all right." The lady spoke with a relaxing voice. "We're calling for help now. They're on the way."

I coughed away at a frantic pace for another ten seconds or so, and then attempted to focus on my surroundings. *What the hell?* Four steering wheels appeared before me.

"Climb in and give him mouth to mouth!" someone shouted from a distance.

"No!" The lady had a take-charge attitude. "He's able to cough, so he's breathing fine. He's starting to catch his breath."

Dizziness and nausea came into the picture. I concentrated and tried to make the four steering wheels morph into one. Cracked glass appeared before me. *I can't move my legs!* My voice scratched. "What's happening?"

"Everything is okay. Help is on the way." The lady's voice came on strong.

The multiple steering wheels merged into one. I found myself in Doug's car. My eyes followed the lady's voice. Her face blurred, and she was upside down. *What the fuck?*

"Can you unbuckle yourself?" a man asked as he squatted to the lady's level.

Pressure intensified in my dome. The windows on all the doors vanished. *Oh shit!* Eyes shot open all the way, and I panicked. "Ahh! What's going on!"

"Stay calm. We're gonna get you outta there." The lady spoke soothingly as she reached into the car to rub my arm.

I had no clue of what happened, but I wanted out of that confined space. My hand snatched and tugged on the forearm of the lady's coat. "Get me outta here!"

Her face mashed against the car door as she moaned, "Oh!"

The man reached in and grabbed my wrist with one hand and the lady's arm with the other. "Whoa! Calm down!"

We struggled for a few seconds, and he separated us. They snatched away and stood up. He wore gym shoes, and she wore women's snow boots.

Panic went up a notch. All I saw was their feet walking beside the ceiling of the car. I stretched my fingers at their ankles, but only grabbed at air. "Help! Don't leave me! Get me out!"

The man squatted and peeked in the car. "Try to calm down. We're gonna get you out of there."

I snagged at his feet. My arm stretched in his direction for a few more seconds until I gave up. I huffed and puffed with all my might as I tried to catch my breath. Freezing air whooshed in one window and breezed out the other. Every joint in my body caught a chill.

The lady crouched down and raised one eyebrow as she glanced inside the car. "Help is already on the way. What's your name?"

All the blood in my body collected at the very top of my head.

My sinuses grew heavy, and my throat clogged. I coughed a few times and pushed the heel of my hand and my wrist against the roof of the car. Most of my weight rested on my arm, and I pressed my back against the seat.

The man repeated his question from earlier. "Can you unbuckle yourself?"

My head thumped as I got a load of the situation. The front dash crunched me in the seat. I could feel my legs, but I could not move them very much. My body hung upside down as if I were frozen at the top of a loop on a roller coaster. The bottom of the dashboard cuffed my thighs like a guardrail. A significant amount of my weight fell on the top on my thighs. The steering wheel angled up and away from me. It missed my chest, but braced me in.

"Don't panic, friend. I'm Detective McMahon. What's your name?" The lady's tone grew more and more friendly.

My tongue restricted the amount of air getting to my lungs. *Oh my God!* A heavy wheeze choked its way from my lungs. I swallowed my spit a couple times and spoke. "Andre!"

"We're gonna get you out of there, Andre," she said.

The man stood up. His feet shuffled around, and he moved away.

I snorted and gagged on more saliva. Extreme fright came over me. I managed to gather the spit in my mouth and swallow.

"Andre, I want you to listen. I need to know if you understand me." The lady's voice flowed like peaceful opera music.

Even though she sounded relaxed, this situation threw me for a loop. "What's happening?"

"You've been in an accident." She came straightforward with the truth as she repositioned herself. "Do you know what city you're in?"

I grew light-headed and confused. *An accident?* Doug, Simone, and the thugs in the car I chased returned to the forefront of my thoughts. *Shit! They got away!* I answered Detective McMahon.

"Yeah, Chicago!"

"Try to relax as much as you can," she said.

The man's feet returned. She stood up straight. I caught another dose of cold air as the hawk swept from window to window.

"We can't move it, or get the doors open." His voice traveled plenty loud enough for me to hear.

"He's trapped in there pretty good," she informed him.

I pressed both palms against the roof of the car and pushed my weight up some. Blood plummeted to my head, and I snorted and coughed up phlegm. I spat in the direction of the passenger side.

Police sirens faded in from the horizon.

"Everything is going to be all right." The lady bent her knees and gazed through the window, raising her eyebrows. "Help is here."

The two spoke to me and reminded me over and over that things would be fine. More police sirens rolled in. Many sets of feet scrambled around outside the car. They defied gravity and strolled around upside down from where I rested.

It grew more difficult to breath. Each inhale and exhale evolved into a heavier wheeze.

"Achoo!" Saliva gathered on the roof of my mouth. Again I spat, but this time most of it rolled up my cheek and dripped into my eye. I wiped my face with the sleeve of my coat. Then I rested as much of the pressure as I could on my other hand. More blood rushed to my head.

"Take this blanket." An arm poked a comforter through the window. The man wore a black leather jacket with the Chicago Police Department patch on the shoulder. "We're gonna get you outta there, Andre."

My elbows wobbled as both my hands pressed against the roof of the car. Shattered glass ripped holes in my gloves. I grabbed the blanket with one hand and tucked it around my back the best I could. My weight rested on one arm.

The officer rose to a stand as a new pair of feet approached along the concrete that appeared to me as the ceiling. Black rubber shoes, black pants, and the bottom of a gray trench coat demanded the attention of all the other ankles. The smaller set of women's snow boots stood by his side. All other feet outside the car paused in place.

"We're gonna have to cut him out," a scratchy voice said.

A fire truck siren faded up in the distance.

My heart thumped away. Every joint in my body shivered as the wind got the best of me. The blood rushing to my head could not be stopped. My toes got numb as the temperature went from freezing, to colder-than-a-muthafucka. The spit gathering at the roof of my mouth and wheezing made for a bad combination. Breathing grew more and more difficult. I spit my saliva to the side. This time, only about twenty-five percent of it rolled up my cheek. I'd long given up on wiping my face.

More sets of feet stormed the scene. Many pairs of black boots and the bottom of orange jump suits took over. *Firemen!* They roamed about the outside of Doug's car bottom side up. One of the men squatted to the window and glanced in. "We're gonna get you outta there, buddy."

The woman's snow boots returned, and she bent next to the firefighter. "You're doing a great job of hanging in there, Andre. We're gonna get you out."

"Hiccup!" It almost got to the point where I wanted to say, *Well, hurry the fuck up and get me outta here, then!* However, they tried to keep me calm. And I would've panicked long before if they weren't there. *"Hiccup!"*

Something grabbed the firefighter's attention, and he darted out of view.

"They're bringing over the jaws of life right now, Andre." The lady kept me posted on the firemen. Next, she tried to make small talk with me. "What do you do?"

"Hiccup!" More saliva collected around my tonsils. I needed to spit, but instead I strained to swallow the glob of slobber. Pain lit up my esophagus as I forced the thick lump through my chest. A small amount of liquid came up my throat and burned the back of my nose. I coughed a few times. After snorting for several seconds to catch my breath, I managed to get out, "I . . . drive . . . the bus."

Petroleum fumes got to my nose.

"Gas is leaking!" a male voice shouted over all other noise. "It's on fire!"

Everyone in boots and orange jump suits scattered along the ceiling, away from the car.

"Hit it with the hose!" one of the firefighters yelled.

McMahon bent over into the window. Timms pulled her away.

"We can't just leave him!" she screamed.

"They need us to clear the area!" Timms replied as he dragged her away.

The commotion outside the car picked up a notch. Everyone's feet scrambled to get away from the ride.

Don't leave me! I gasped and hissed away, trapped upside down with my hands pressed against the roof. The gas odor grew stronger. *What's happening, now?*

Two seconds later, Doug's car exploded.

BOOM!

Chapter Fourteen:
Detective Timms

The car lifted off the ground and hovered in the air for a full second. The Escort crashed and skidded a few feet. *Oh shit! The car blew up!*

Fear kicked in right away. My sense of having no control skyrocketed. I bounced around some more. My neck and head wobbled out of control. The seat belt worked overtime as it held me in the driver seat.

Heat crept in at my feet, along the back of my legs, and on my ass. Sort of a welcomed feeling after being stranded in the cold for so long. An orange glare reflected off the concrete outside the window.

The car stopped moving. McMahon flew into view out of nowhere. She landed on her chest and slid the rest of the way to the window. Her head stuck inside. "Andre! Are you okay?"

I coughed a few times and replied, "Yeah, I think so."

A stream of ice-cold water blasted the driver side door. It splattered in every direction and stormed down on McMahon. The water ricocheted about the car and crashed into my face.

My forearms came together in front of my grill in self-defense.

Chills rushed from head to toe.

The water pressure let up, and I relaxed my arms. McMahon unfolded her body from a ball and glanced into the car at me. Smaller splashes of liquid smashed against our faces as the firefighters shot the hose at the fire.

I hung at a different angle with more room to move. My legs shifted around more.

McMahon came to her knees and tugged at the door. "It's open!"

The metal cracked a few times. The door unfastened and scraped against the ground.

I was able to twist around some. The dashboard and steering wheel gave way. My left leg wiggled through additional space created by the blast.

She came to her feet and reached through the door for me.

I grabbed onto her with one hand and the other gripped the bottom of the car. My body moved as I tugged myself in her direction. I braced one foot on the car and tried to climb out, but everything came to a halt. My other leg locked in place.

Water pounded the car and drenched me from head to toe. Below zero temperatures ate away at me while heat surrounded my foot.

"Wait!" I jerked away from McMahon and scooted my upper body into the car. One leg was surrounded by metal. "I can't get outta here. It's got me!"

Detective Timms appeared out of nowhere. He yelled, "Get those jaws of life over here, now!"

Two firefighters carried a huge metal pair of scissors with a long cord extending from it. The detectives moved out the way. A couple firemen held the cord, and a few others crowded around. Water bounced all over the place.

It's freezing! I shivered uncontrollably and sneezed away.

They inserted the jaws of life into the bent up clutter of steel and clamped down on what was soon to be scrap metal. The steel snapped like a toothpick. The scissors opened and clenched onto the car in a different spot. It crunched through the ride with ease, and they pulled the metal apart.

Relief struck me. I grabbed the door to pull myself out the car.

The firefighters snatched me up and virtually lifted me from the wreckage. I swung my body around and staggered to my feet, stumbling along the pavement hunched over. They tossed a blanket over me the same way they used to toss a cape across James Brown during his concerts. My knees wobbled and jiggled like spaghetti. Water sprayed at Doug's car as it rested upside down in a vacant lot near an eighteen wheeler. The wind whooshed through every bone in my body.

My teeth chattered like a cartoon character. I'd literally never experienced anything like that in my entire life. Every muscle in my body tightened and vibrated like a hummingbird. Most of my weight leaned on the two firefighters. They led me to an ambulance a few yards away where a bright orange spine board lay on the ground. My legs gave way, and they directed me to the dirt beside the plank. I dropped to the ground.

"Rest on your back." A paramedic guided me to the ground as he took the blanket off me. "Lie straight and try not to move."

I attempted to do exactly what he said, but it proved to be impossible. My body trembled like a saltshaker suspended over an order of fries. *"Achoo! Hiccup!"* My throat grew sore, and I sneezed away. *"Achoo!"* I rolled to lie flat on my back, but I could not stop shaking. My eyes focused on the sky.

One EMT dropped to her knees above me. She placed her palms over my ears on both sides of my head as her fingers tightened and poked into my collarbones. A different technician squatted and grabbed my wrist.

"Pulse is present!" He pressured my inner arm with his middle and forefinger. Then he did the same with the other arm. "Pulse is present! Can you move your fingers?"

I jiggled my digits the best I could.

He duck walked to the end of my limbs and verified a pulse in my toes. "Can you move your feet?"

I followed instructions again.

A third paramedic came out of nowhere with a cervical collar. He ripped apart the Velcro and slipped it under my neck. The first technician held my head still as the collar fastened under my chin. Two other techs reached across and braced me alongside my body. They rolled me on my side ninety degrees as someone else slid the spine board up under me.

"Do you know what city you're in?" the female EMT holding my head asked.

The detective asked the same thing earlier. I recalled the question, but no longer could I remember the answer. *What's going on?* Confusion set in. My head thumped as they placed me on the board. I shifted a little to climb onto it and did my best to stay still. However, every joint in my body ached and quivered nonstop. One side of my face rested against an orange brace. They secured my head in position on the other side with a brace just like it.

"He's turning blue!" The man over my torso strapped down my upper body. "We're dealing with hypothermia . . . those wet clothes have got to go!"

"We need to hurry and get him on the bus!" The other tech fastened my legs to the board. "Lift him on three. One . . . two . . . three!"

They boosted me and the board off the ground and placed me on a stretcher. I felt every bump on the ground as they wheeled me to the emergency vehicle. Ambulance lights flashed and rotated all over the place. They got me off the ground and into the back of the wagon.

The three techs climbed on board, and the door shut behind them. Heat blasted from multiple angles like an oven. They stripped off their outer coats. One held my board straight, while the other two grabbed scissors and snipped away at my clothes. They carefully slipped them from under me and exposed my butt naked body.

I shivered away as they tossed blankets over me. My vision blurred, and everything moved in slow motion.

"His blood pressure is low." The female updated the rest of the crew. She attempted to get a thermometer in my mouth. "His teeth are chattering away. I can't get it in."

"Try to put it under his arm," a different EMT suggested. "Here, I'll hold him."

They kept me in place as she slipped the device between my skin.

"His pressure is still dropping!" The other technician gave his input.

The ambulance siren roared as we glided through the Chicago streets. I grew sick to my stomach.

Everything went black.

* * * * *

Beep . . . Beep . . . Beep . . .

Light crept in little by little. Everything blurred before me. It took a few seconds to focus, but an image formed in front of my eyes.

Colisa appeared with a soft smile and her eyebrows narrowed. The smile grew larger. "Hey."

Where am I? I got a load of my surroundings and found myself in a hospital room with a pale green gown wrapped around my otherwise naked body. An IV dripped fluid into my arm. Monitors beeped and flashed red and green numbers. *What's going on?*

"You are okay." She must've recognized the expression on my face. "You were in an accident."

An accident? My mind raced for a few seconds. Right away I recalled the car chase, the accident, and the authorities pulling me out the car.

Colisa leaned into the bed and hugged me around my head. Her heartbeat banged through her breasts and crashed against my face. Mad comfort sunk in from the familiar bosom. I leaned into her and took a deep breath. My toes, fingers, and legs tingled. More thoughts shot through my head. I jerked away from her and sat up. "Doug! Is he okay?"

She made eye contact with me as she flashed a broken smile. "He's alive."

My heart thumped a bit quicker. The monitors beeped faster. *Simone!* "That kid! Oh shit, Colisa. That young brotha's dead because of me."

"I left the baby with Dorian and came right down as soon as they called." She hugged me tighter. "What happened, Andre?"

Damn! My eyes watered as I sat up and pulled away from her. "Everything went wrong. We just wanted to talk to him for a second. Where's Doug?"

"He's . . . here." She paused, acting like there was something to hide. "They have him in a different room."

"I've gotta see him." I sat up the rest of the way and grabbed at the IV in my arm. "Take this thing off of me."

"No, wait!" Colisa snatched away at my wrist. "Let the nurse do that!"

I ignored her, and we tussled over the tubes in my arm. The door opened, and three people marched in. An Asian man led the way in a white lab coat. Colisa and I paused and gazed at the intruders. A man in a gray overcoat and an athletically built woman followed.

"Hello, Andre. I'm Dr. Lin." He posed at the end of the bed with two other people beside him. "This is Detectives Timms and McMahon. They have a few questions to ask you."

"Detectives? Wait, am I okay?" The tingling in my fingertips and toes subsided. "My arms and legs felt asleep a second ago."

"You're looking pretty good," Dr. Lin replied. "You caught a moderate case of hypothermia, but we got your body temperature back to normal. We're gonna observe you for twenty-four hours just to be safe."

I glanced at the detectives as I grabbed for the tube in my arm. "I'd love to chat, but I gotta find my boy, Doug."

"Just try to relax," Colisa said, getting in the way of me removing the IV.

"Doug's told me a lot about you." Detective Timms filled me in. "One of the suspects referred to your group as Suburban Old Men."

I froze in my tracks. Only Doug, that goon, and I heard Stallion Pee say that. *How does this guy know?* I made eye contact with the detective. "How do you know Doug?"

"For years before McMahon and I worked together, he used to be my partner." His voice scratched like he smoked squares his entire life. "He told me you guys are working on this case together."

I gave this guy a once over from head to toe. Soon, I recognized the lady. She helped to keep me from panicking while I was trapped under Doug's car. Also, these were two of the detectives that questioned us at the murder scene.

"I'm gonna step away." Dr. Lin headed to the door. "The nurse will be in to prep you for a CT scan."

Colisa used both her hands to grab mine. "Do you want me stay?"

Usually, I'd want her by my side in just about any situation. A big part of me wanted her to remain next to me at that moment. But I couldn't trust that these detectives wouldn't mention too much about Antoinette Miller. I made eye contact with my wife. "It's okay, sweetheart. I'll be fine. Go call Dorian and check on

Linda. Let 'em know I'm okay."

She kissed me on the lips.

My eyes never left the detectives as she left the room. I got another load of the two figures at the end of my bed and said the appropriate thing. "Thanks for saving my life tonight."

"Don't mention it." McMahon came with the cool, relaxing voice. "You hung in there under some tough circumstances. I don't know if I would've been so calm if I were in your place."

"Seems like you had a pretty eventful night." Detective Timms stated the obvious. They both paused, and an awkward moment of silence endured.

That's not a question, but they're waiting for a response. I'll play along. "Yes, detective. Very eventful. What do you know about the suspect that called us Suburban Old Men?"

"Enough that I don't think he committed this crime." Detective Timms finally got to his point. "We suspect a member of the Vice Lords pulled the trigger."

My mind shot to the conversation Doug and I had while staking out the bus stop. His voice echoed in my head. *My old partner is a good cop. Last night, he let me know they don't think this was done by the GDs. They think the Vice Lords did it.* My curiosity popped off. "What makes you think that?"

"The information you gave us at the murder scene. The killer tossed Molotov cocktails on the roof at you." Timms circled something on his notepad. "This is the fourth time in the last three months a crime was committed and at least one Molotov cocktail was involved. Each other instance involved the Vice Lords."

"It appears the young man that died tonight may have known some information that could've helped solve the case." McMahon's voice could have possibly swayed a fish to buy a glass of ice water. "Is there anything you can share to help get to the bottom of this?"

"I'm so pissed off and disappointed about what happened to Simone. Unfortunately, he didn't get the chance to give us anything." Disbelief and shock sank in a bit deeper. I pictured him gagging on his own blood in my arms. My homeboy didn't look too good either. "Wait! Where is Doug? Really? How is he?"

Detectives Timms and McMahon glanced at each other.

"He lost a lot of blood." McMahon filled me in with her soft voice, but what she said didn't sit well with me. "He went into shock and lost consciousness."

My heart dropped. I sprung up and sat at full attention. "What?"

"They restored his blood pressure with a transfusion," she said, "but he has not awakened."

The heart monitor beeped at a much faster pace. Panic came over me. "Where is he? I want to see him! Right now!"

"He's in the Intensive Care Unit," Detective Timms responded.

I swung my legs around and snatched the bed remote. The call button went down multiple times as my thumb crashed into it. I yelled into the speaker, "Get this needle out my arm, and take me to see Doug, pronto!"

The nurse's voice amplified through the remote, *"Wait, be careful!"*

Detective Timms and McMahon stumbled over one another to try to keep me from pulling the IV out my arm. Colisa and a nurse stormed in and joined the effort to calm me down. They agreed to take me to see Doug once I relaxed. I slipped on pajama bottoms, socks, and house shoes my wife brought with her. She tossed another hospital gown over my back.

The nurse led the way down the hall as I rolled the IV along the floor. Detectives Timms and McMahon flanked me along with Colisa. We made our way to an opposite wing of the hospital on the same floor. The nurse pointed me into Doug's room. Everyone else waited outside.

Doug rested in a hospital bed with a huge oxygen tube down

his throat. Way more monitors beeped in his room and made mechanical type noises. Wires and IVs were attached to him in several different places and one of them was clipped to his forefinger. Three teary-eyed people sat by his bedside. They glanced up at me at the same time.

"Oh, I'm sorry." I assumed they were his family as my heart thumped. Seeing Doug lying there unconscious left me speechless. I stepped backward and glided out the room in disbelief. The IV pole stood tall beside me as I questioned the nurse. "What's the deal with him?"

"He lost a few pints of blood so fast that hypovolemic shock kicked in." The nurse spoke with confidence and tact. "The doctors repaired his shoulder, but he's not responding neurologically."

"What does all that mean?" I asked. "Is he gonna be okay?"

"His brain was deprived of oxygen for quite a while," she replied. "Only time will tell."

This news devastated me. My mind bounced around out of control. I posed in front of the others and made eye contact with everyone. They stared back at me in silence.

The nurse said, "It's time we get you ready for your CT scan."

"Okay." I headed to my room as I grabbed my wife's hand. The events of the previous few days danced through my mind. I stopped and turned to face Detective Timms. "This is too dangerous, and I got too much to lose. I'm not doing this anymore."

Detectives Timms and McMahon glanced at one another.

"That's a smart move," Timms replied.

"Simone didn't get a chance to ID the shooter, but he let us know it wasn't Stallion Pee." I told the detectives what I thought would help. The information did me no good any longer. Plus, it confirmed their theory that the Gangster Disciples were not responsible for these crimes. "Whoever did this drive-by wore red.

They definitely ain't Folks."

Detective Timms jotted down the information on his notepad. They thanked us and remained at Doug's room to console his family. Colisa stayed by my side like a soldier and waited for me as they did the CT scan and ran other tests. Meanwhile, I filled her in on the case and most of the things Doug and I went through. My health checked out fine, but they insisted I remain in hospital care for a full twenty-four hours. I eventually convinced Colisa to go home to take care of herself and the family. She left, but promised to return to stay the night with me.

Once she bounced out of the hospital, relief came over me. I finally got a chance to speak to the doctor alone. Next time he stepped in, I got at him. "Doctor Lin, can you test me for STDs?"

Chapter Fifteen:
Partners in Crime

Both the silent treatment and the attitude lifted. Colisa catered to my every need. The nurse wheeled me out the front door, and I climbed into the passenger seat under my own power. The sun shined brightly on the first day above freezing in over a week. The temperature hit forty degrees that morning. Colisa guided her navy blue Honda CR-V through traffic. Three news vans parked along our block. Reporters yelled questions from the sidewalk, and cameras pointed at us as we pulled through them and into the driveway. The garage door shut behind us. Dorian and Linda smiled our way as we strolled in from the garage and entered the living room.

"Daddy!" My baby girl jumped into my arms. "Yay!"

"Hey pumpkin!" I smiled ear to ear as I tossed her into the stratosphere and caught her with both hands.

"What happened?" Linda asked. "Dorian said you were sick."

"Yes, daddy was at the doctor for a couple of nights." My shoulder ached after chucking her in the air. *Glad I didn't drop her.* I set her down and held her hand as we strolled to the kitchen. "But I feel a lot better now."

"Good, daddy. I missed you." She skipped beside me and cheesed away. "Can we play Candy Land?"

"Not right now, Linda." Colisa trailed behind us alongside Dorian. She reasoned with our daughter using her 'mommy' voice. "Daddy's a little tired, and we have to let him get some rest. Maybe later."

Purple balls wrapped Linda's two ponytails close to her scalp. An immaculate part went down the middle of her head, and the perfect amount of oil sheen on her hair glistened in the light. Purple and pink barrettes dangled off the ends of her twists. Her eyebrows went up as far as they could go. "We gonna play *today?*"

I smiled. "I'm gonna think about it, sweetheart."

"Hey, wanna play on my computer?" Dorian jumped in the conversation with perfect timing. Playing on Dorian's computer served as the ultimate distraction when we needed to keep her occupied. He headed in the direction of his room and gave a 'c'mon' head nod to Linda. "We can pull up Dora the Explorer."

"Yes!" Linda jerked away from me and sprinted to catch up with Dorian. She grabbed his hand and hopped toward the stairs.

I smirked. *Look at my baby girl.*

"You doing okay?" Colisa asked as she opened the fridge and glanced inside.

"Yes. Surprisingly, I feel fine." I grabbed a couple glasses from the cabinet. "A scratch here and there, as you already know. These burns are still the worse thing I got going."

"This is the first time Linda's woke up in this house without being able to lay eyes on her daddy." Colisa grabbed a pitcher of pink lemonade Kool-Aid and closed the fridge. "She asked a billion questions."

"Well, now it seems like she's back to normal." I pulled out a chair and parked it at the kitchen table. The two glasses rested in front of me. *Doug's still in the hospital.* "I wish I can say the same for everybody."

"I wish they would take that tube outta his throat." She filled our glasses three-fourths of the way to the top. "It looks like he can breathe on his own."

"Yeah, but he's not waking up." My conscience placed the responsibility of the events on the man in the mirror. *That young dude is dead.* "Simone's family will probably want to kill me when they find out the real reason he followed us to the car."

"C'mon, Andre. Don't stress yourself out about that." She returned the pitcher to the fridge. "In the papers and in the news, it sounds like the police are covering up information about you guys like your friend Doug is still a cop. There was a shotgun in the car, right? As far as I know, they haven't mentioned that once."

"Yeah, I noticed that, too. And that's a good thing . . . at least for now. I bet they're keeping everything on the low while they work the case. Stallion Pee would be locked up under the jailhouse right now if it were up to the press." I took a sip from my glass. "I'm gonna go back to the hospital to check on Doug later. But first, I'm gonna get some rest."

"We both need some sleep, but I'm supposed to be at Momma's house today." Colisa sauntered to the counter and grabbed the notepad beside the phone. "You have a lot of messages. TV and radio stations keep calling. Your friends Kyle and Greg called, and your union rep from the job. Also, Antoinette Miller called here three times."

Antoinette Miller? That name coming from my wife's mouth took me by surprise. I spit out my Kool-Aid, and it sprayed across the kitchen table.

"Are you okay?" Colisa asked.

Gotta play this off. I set the glass on the table and coughed once or twice to make it look good. "I'm fine. It just went down the wrong pipe."

"Oh, okay." She grabbed her glass and tapped me across the back a few times. "That's the lady who hired Doug, right?"

"Yeah, right." *Does Antoinette know he's in the hospital?* I went for the paper towels to wipe the table down. "She's gonna have to get someone else to help find who killed her son."

Colisa took a few steps away. She paused for three seconds then faced me. A soft smile came across her face. She obviously was trying to have a moment. "I'm glad you're okay."

"Thanks, babe." I returned her stare.

"I've seen a lot of things in you over the last couple of weeks," she said.

Oh lawd, here we go again with this. My eyelids shut as my eyeballs rolled to the back of my head.

"You're a very brave man. I've always known this." She shifted her weight to one leg. "And you usually try to do the right thing."

I did not expect her to say that. *She thinks I'm brave, huh? Yeah, still got it.* But I knew a 'but' was on the way.

"However, you have a family, and we don't want you to get hurt." She spoke with a soft tone. "Linda, Dorian, and I should rank a lot higher than you just wanting to solve some mystery. Especially, when it's not even your *real* job."

"Uncle Dre!" Dorian yelled down from the top of the stairs.

I stood there speechless. Every bone in my body wanted to get defensive and snap back, but she spoke the truth.

"I'm not trying to trip," Colisa whispered. She spoke loud enough so only I heard her. "Just remember who'll be hurt if something *really* happens to you."

Dorian's voice rang down again. "Uncle Dre!"

Colisa marched away to the living room.

"Yeah?" I yelled up the stairs.

"Come here! You're on *World Star!*" he replied.

What the heck is this kid talking about? I finished wiping the table and glided up the stairs. His bedroom door opened. I stepped into his area expecting marijuana to hit me in the nose. My chest filled with air, but all I smelled was air freshener. I glanced around the room and noticed my baby girl fast asleep on his bed. *Oh.*

"Uncle Dre, check this out!" Dorian lamped in his favorite chair and manipulated his laptop. He tapped the mouse pad as he handed me his computer.

I flipped it around, and a video rolled before my eyes.

"The action for the Golden Era Hip-Hop crew Inner City Youth continues to hit the fan. Andre Johnson crashed a Ford Escort into an eighteen wheeler." The reporter spoke over footage of the wreckage from the accident. *"He was rushed to St. Bernard Hospital on Chicago's South Side where he was examined and released. That's a miracle considering the sight of this scrap metal. Inner City Youth front man Ichabod Crane had this to say:*

"Dr. Dre and his family are going through a lot." Kyle's face cut onto the screen with a serious look. *"I just hope the media can respect their privacy right now."*

"The accident comes just days after a triple homicide and apparent arson attack took place during their recent performance." The reporter's voice returned. A camera phone image of me leaving the concert crime scene and heading through the parking lot took over the screen. They zoomed in on the torched bottom of my pants legs. *"With the murders at this event, and the drive-by shooting of college student Simone Manney, Chicago's homicide count hit forty-seven for the month of January."*

I shook my head in disbelief. *Shit wasn't this bad in the Al Capone days.*

"What's the deal with the Hip-Hop scene in Chicago? Endoscope Records recording artist Stallion Pee continues to have legal woes." Footage of a cop guiding Stallion Pee's head into a police car hit the screen. Handcuffs locked his hands behind his back. *"Police took him into custody for parole violations. His people could not be reached for comment."*

The video clip ended. I raised one eyebrow as I handed the laptop to Dorian. "If I didn't know any better and I saw that, I would think Stallion Pee was guilty all the way."

"He's not, huh?" Dorian asked as he grabbed his computer. He spoke in a soft voice so as not to wake the baby. "What's the rest of the story, Uncle Dre?"

"We're gonna leave that up to the police." I grabbed the other seat in the room. "I've had enough of playing cops and robbers."

"Aunt Lisa said you went to college with the guy that's still in the hospital." Dorian placed his computer on his nightstand. "How'd you know old boy who got killed?"

Guilt struck me hard, again. I paused to gather myself. "He used to ride my bus. That's a pretty tragic end to a young life."

"I know, right? It kinda made me think about a lot of stuff." My nephew rotated his seat to face me. "Aunt Lisa and I talked about a few things. I'm not gonna smoke weed in the house anymore."

"Oh, okay." I never thought it to be a big deal. The only thing that stopped me from smoking myself was my job. "Well, that's a good thing. I'm glad y'all talked."

"I heard your old song on the radio twice yesterday," Dorian said with a sense of pride. He scooted his seat across the room and flipped on the TV.

That caught me off guard. "Really?"

"Yep. People want to talk to you to find out what's going on." He tapped the game console and the TV screen lit up. "You get your phone messages?"

Dorian and I shot the breeze for a few more moments as he played his video game. My baby girl remained asleep, and I stepped away to return at least two of those messages. I grabbed the horn off the wall in the kitchen and hit up a three-way call with my boys, Kyle and Greg.

"The news been talkin' about that accident nonstop." Kyle showed concern in his voice. "How you holdin' up?"

"Apparently, I have good people covering my back with the

press." Sarcasm flowed from my voice. "So I'm straight. You're like the spokesman of the year, right?"

He laughed. "People are blowin' us up, and we had to check on you, man."

Greg jumped in. "Yeah, we had to make sure you're all good. Colisa let us know you're still alive. I hope your boy, Doug pulls through."

"Wow, thank y'all for the concern." I shook my head as the reality struck me again. "I hope that dude pulls through, too."

"Man, if you need anything just let us know," Kyle said.

Greg added, "Yeah, just holla' at us."

I filed that offer away in the back of my mind.

Colisa and I climbed in the bed and took the nap of all naps. She woke up first and got herself and Linda together. They headed to my mother-in-law's. A couple hours later, I sprung awake and got up on the last of the oxtail stew. Before returning to the hospital, I gave my union rep a buzz.

"Thanks for calling me back." Kevin Payne worked for the CTA for eleven years and represented the driver's union. "I've been sitting by the phone waiting. I'm glad you're okay."

"Thanks, man. It was a heck of an experience." I guessed the accident to be the main topic of gossip at the job. "Is this about the extra couple of days I took off? I should have plenty of sick time piled up."

"No, Andre." Disappointment came through his voice. "It's about your toxicology screening."

I frowned and jerked my head back. "My toxicology screening? What could possibly be wrong with that?"

The new law required drug testing for city bus drivers whenever we had an accident. The CTA took a sample of blood at the hospital. I wrote it off to being part of the routine.

"They discovered marijuana in your system," he said.

What the . . . Marijuana? This blew me away. "But I ain't

smoked no weed in years. That's impossible!"

The union rep went on about 'post-accident testing' and 'controlled substances testing procedures.'

The wheels of my brain rotated away. *How could I fail a drug test? For weed?* Then it hit me. I pictured myself in closed areas sitting beside Dorian when he smoked and puffed his blunts. The deep breaths I took while he exhaled in my face may as well have been shotguns. *Shit!*

Kevin's voice shifted to a matter of fact tone. "There's more. The report showed your system full of GSRA."

GSRA? A light bulb the size of the moon went off in my head. "Wait a minute! What's that?"

"Genetic Suppression Relief Antidotes." He came off like he knew what he was talking about. "This is only the second time this drug has come up on a test for a CTA employee."

The bulb evolved into a huge spotlight, and it shined on MC ET's last tweet: *#RegalTheater GSRA out back.* My heart raced out of control. *What's really going on?* I cleared my throat. "To be honest with you, Kev, I've never even heard of that."

"Most people haven't. It pops up here and there in our city and in Houston," he said. "It's the stuff they let the astronauts use in space. Sometimes it leaks to the streets and is sold as a recreational drug. It could even be used on men for date rape. The only known places that make it are NASA and the University of Chicago."

Bells, chimes, and whistles went off. *Antoinette Miller!* Her voice echoed loud and clear. *That's way stronger than Vicodin. That's the stuff they let the astronauts play with.* Rage ripped through my chest as the images returned to my memory. *I've been working for the University of Chicago for almost twenty years now. I'm a nurse. Remember?* I wasted no time placing my next call.

She answered on the second ring.

I went right in on her. "Bitch, you drugged me?"

Chapter Sixteen:
Genetic Suppression Relief Antidotes

"What?" Confusion came through in her voice. "What are you talking about?"

"You know just what the hell I'm talkin' about!" No way would I let her deny this. "The red pills. You set them out in front of me, knowing I would take one."

"Oh no!" She did her best to act surprised. "You took one of the red pills?"

"Don't play dumb with me!" My eyebrows came together in anger. I wanted to jump through the phone. "Why Antoinette? Why would you do that to me? You know I'm a married man."

She sniffled a few times. I could virtually hear the crocodile tears rolling down her cheeks. "I'm really sorry, Andre. Really, I didn't mean for you to take a red pill."

"Bullshit!" Steam came out my nose and ears. My scalp flew off my head and hit the ceiling. "You knew just what the fuck you were doing, bitch!"

"Now, wait a minute!" She sobbed and made a dramatic pause. I could feel her neck rotating through the phone. "I'm not gone be too many more bitches!"

"Whatever Antoinette. Just tell me what the hell's going on here?" I paced back and forth about the kitchen with the phone glued to my ear. "What's with the GSRA popping up in my system? That shit's only made where you work. Your son's last tweet had something to do with GSRA. Stop playing with me, girl. What's going on?"

A moment of silence hit the phone. She whimpered some more and bawled loud enough so I could hear.

This chick can still make the river flow at the drop of a dime. My patience wore thin. I let her cry for a few seconds and then said, "I'm waiting."

"You're right, Andre . . . there's a lot more to the story." Her hesitation frustrated me to death. "There's a lot more, and you deserve to know the truth. The longer I keep it from you, the harder it gets."

"This got me fucked up, girl." The suspense killed me. "Spit it out."

"This has to be said in person," she replied.

"Stop playin' with me, Antoinette!"

"No, seriously. This is something that can't be repeated over the phone."

A frustration headache clobbered my dome. I wiped my palm across my eyes, nose, mouth, and chin. "I'm not about to come to your house."

"And I'm not about to invite you." She showed no hesitation with her comeback. "You sound too angry, and I'm scared to be alone with you. Let's meet at a public place."

Antoinette and I agreed to link up at Evergreen Plaza on 95th and Western. I washed up and tossed on a gray workout suit with gray low top Nikes. The keys hit my hand, and my nephew met me in the kitchen as I held my coat.

He caught me by surprise. I said, "Dorian?"

"It's me in the flesh, Uncle Dre. Can I roll?" He refused to give up.

"Sorry, son." I felt bad rejecting him, but my focus rested on getting some answers. "You've gotta sit this one out, again."

"C'mon, Uncle Dre?" His eyebrows pulled together like a sad puppy. "I know it's a lot going on. Let me roll. I wanna help."

"Not now, Dorian." I wrapped up in my coat and gloves as I stormed through the dining room and into the garage.

The sun beamed through clear skies with no wind. I had a chance to breathe as I broamed my way to the Southside mall. Anger boiled inside me, but I took a moment to relax. *Try not to choke the shit outta her.* I parked in a lower level parking lot around back and strolled into the center square of the mall. Leisurely, I scanned the bottom floor first, but then swept across the upper level and caught a glimpse of her.

Our eyes connected as I glided up the escalator. She met me in front of Spencer's. We faced each other in the middle of the mall as dozens and dozens of people went on with their business surrounding us.

She clutched her purse close to her body. "Have you been to see Doug today?"

That caught me off guard. "How'd you know he's in the hospital?"

"Your accident is national news. Plus, I've always kept in touch with his sister online. We spoke earlier." Her eyes surveyed the mall as she maintained conversation with me. "She's keeping me posted, but I haven't heard from her since this morning."

"That was the last chance I had to check on him, myself. I haven't been back up there." I stepped out the way and pulled her to the side as a man looking down at his cell phone almost walked right through us. "So what's the story that can't be repeated over the phone?"

"Maybe we should have a seat." She strolled to a group of cushioned couches near the food court.

I followed her, stopping once to allow space for a kid carrying a balloon to sprint past.

She copped a squat with her back to a teenager speaking on her phone. Antoinette's palm pat the open space on the couch beside her.

"No thank you." I posed with my arms crossed. "I'd rather stand."

Her eyes watered a little. She pulled a couple Kleenex from her purse and caught her tears before they ran down her face. "I'm really sorry, Andre."

I braced myself for a performance worthy of an Academy Award. My lips twisted to the side. "What exactly are you sorry about?"

"I'm sorry you took one of the red ones."

She can't be serious. I stared daggers into her. "You knew exactly what you were doing."

"Wait, let me rephrase that." She peeked over her shoulders one at a time. "I'm sorry I brought the red ones out. I shouldn't have presented them to you in the first place."

"You're right about that, Antoinette." Not the exact apology I wanted. However, it made sense a little for some strange reason. Nobody forced me to take the red pill. *But she knew what she was doing. Don't lose focus.* I tried to speak in a firm tone without raising my voice. "It *would* be all good, but you took advantage of my state of mind. You had sex with me."

"I know . . . I shouldn't have done that." She rubbed the palm of her hand against her forehead. "It's just that . . . you were threatening to leave, and you weren't gonna help find Eric's killer anymore. I panicked and took advantage of you. Please forgive me."

"It's not that easy, sistah." No way would I give in to her soft voice and her weeping like she's the victim. "I ain't tryin' to get caught up in your emotions. I'm looking for the connection. The reason I'm here is to get the real deal. Eric's last entry on Twitter . . . tell me about it."

"My son's last tweet?" She frowned and blinked in confusion a few times. "I don't know what he meant. That's what I need you to find out."

"Don't gimme that, Antoinette!" My heart rate sped up. Fury erupted inside of me. *I've had enough of this chick!* My voice went up. "Look, playtime is over. Tell me about GSRA. Right here. Right now!"

The girl sitting on the other side of Antoinette grabbed her shopping bag off the floor in front of her. She strolled away, never removing the cell phone from her ear.

Antoinette scooted over to make more room for me. "Please, have a seat. This is something you need to hear."

I took a deep breath and glanced around the mall. After a dramatic pause of my own, I relaxed beside her. "I'm trying to be real patient with you, Antoinette. You didn't tell us everything. What's going on?"

"I know how this must look," she said. "But Eric didn't know anything about GSRA as far as I know. I was surprised when Doug brought the message to my attention."

I asked the obvious question. "Why didn't you tell us what it stood for?"

"Because I wasn't sure that's what Eric meant. I'm still not certain, and I want to know what's going on just as much as you do." She took a breath and glanced at her surroundings. "That's why I called Doug. I couldn't tell the police Eric potentially sent a message to the world about a top secret government drug, when I wasn't sure that's the case. That would've cost me my job. Hell, I couldn't even tell you and Doug."

"No, that's not a good enough reason to keep it from us." Her logic didn't sit well with me. "It's not making any sense. Don't you think it would've been nice if Doug and I knew there was the possibility of a connection?"

"Probably so, but I was just worried about my job . . . my career . . . and going to jail." Her reply seemed sincere enough. "I really hope the message my son sent has nothing to do with the University of Chicago. And that's the truth."

"Who else knows this?"

"I don't know . . ." She delayed speaking for a few seconds, as someone strolled in front of us. "Are you gonna find out who killed Eric?"

"No." My eyes cut away from hers. I stared in the opposite direction. "You expect me to risk my life for you after you drugged me?"

"I didn't drug you, Andre."

"Call it what you wanna. I'm done." I rose from the couch and stepped a few paces away. "I don't trust you, so I can't deal. You can threaten to tell my wife whatever you want."

"No, wait!" She sprung up and bolted ahead to cut me off. "Don't leave!"

"I'm sorry." Her presence pissed me off. I stepped around her. "Get out my way with your slick, high-yellow ass. You had me come down here thinking you had some type of connection to talk about. Then I get here, and you tell me the exact opposite."

She grabbed my arm and pleaded with me. "Hold it. Wait! There's something you should know!"

"Oh, you got somethin' else to add, huh?" My voice got loud as I yanked my arm away. "Don't touch me!"

She closed her eyes and inhaled. They opened as she released the breath. She gazed up at me. A smile plastered on her face as she sang through her teeth. "We're getting loud, and people are looking at us."

I glanced around and caught several people watching. One lady literally focused in with all her might as she ate popcorn. I guided Antoinette to the couch, and we both had a seat.

"You get sixty seconds." I wanted no further parts of her. She had my attention for what I hoped to be the last time. "What is it, Antoinette? What more do you have to say?"

She appeared as if she had a bad report card, and she was scared to show it to her parents. "I wish you weren't so angry."

As much as I wanted to explode, I remained calm. I stared her down without saying a thing. She had the floor, and I was out of there when she finished saying what she had to say.

Her eyebrows came together all the way. Tears spilled down her cheeks. She blotted her face with tissue as her eyes reached bloodshot red. "There's no easy way to put this. And I'm so sorry for keeping it from you."

I pulled my cheeks in and raised one eyebrow.

"I'm searching for the right words." Two small pieces of tissue clung to her face. "Okay, here it goes . . ."

Frustration kicked in. "I suggest you hurry, and do it quickly."

"It's about Eric." She closed her eyes for a tick. More tears flushed out as she reopened them. "He was your son."

Chapter Seventeen:
My Son

Time froze. I rewound her statement in my mind and replayed it three times. *He was your son. He was your son. He was your son.*

Antoinette and I had sex for a sixth time the night before my wedding. We bumped into each other at a club in the middle of my bachelor celebration. I told myself it was fate and gave in to my cold feet. My body exclusively belonged to my wife for the following nineteen years.

"I'm sorry, Andre. I wanted to tell you a long time ago, but you got married," she pleaded, to gain my understanding. "I'm sorry."

A calculator went off in my head. I tried to subtract MC ET's age from the current year.

"He was born forty-one weeks after the night of your bachelor party." She sobbed as she shared the math. "I didn't know how to tell you and your new wife about your accidental child."

No. My mouth dropped to the ground. I couldn't move a muscle. *She's comin' with this after all these years?*

"So, please, Andre." She sniffed a few times and blew her nose.

"I need you to find out who killed *our* son."

"Wow, Antoinette." Shock swept through me. *Oh, this is supposed to be OUR son now?* "You can't be serious about this."

She grabbed my wrist. "I know this is a lot to soak in."

"You damn right it's a lot to soak in!" I snatched away from her and came to my feet. "How you just gone throw some shit in my face like that?"

"I didn't know what to do!" She shot to her feet and begged me to stay. "Please, Andre. He was our son."

"You drop a bomb on me at a moment like this, and you expect me to believe you?" Her track record showed no credibility. But mathematics told a different story. I didn't know which side to lean toward. Anger ripped through my body as I strolled away from her. "I can't be near you right now."

She bolted in front of me to cut me off again. "Don't walk away. I've been going crazy for years with this in my head."

I grabbed her by her shoulders and shook the hell out of her. "You're disrupting my life. Would you just leave me alone!"

Her voice shrieked. The body gyrated in rhythm with her cries. "No, don't do this!"

I released her. She stumbled backward and bawled out of control. Tears plummeted down her cheeks. She sulked away and wiped her face with her bare hands. The crowd gawked at me like they'd just spotted the number one most wanted criminal in the universe.

I took two steps in reverse. While scanning the area, I noticed no camera phones pointing at me. However, I knew they would pop out soon if I didn't get out of there. My palms reached for the sky.

"Move on, folks. Nothing to see here." I dropped my hands and summoned as much sarcasm as I could muster. "It's okay. She's my dead baby's momma."

She grabbed for me as she stood in one place. "Please, don't go!"

I ignored her and stormed away. The shades came out my pocket and hit my face as I made it to the parking lot. My imagination took off about my nephew pulling up a clip of that last scene on his computer. *I gotta check myself in public going forward.* The truck got me out of there and took me north on Western Avenue.

He was your son. I cruised at thirty miles per hour with the heat on medium-low. Rush hour traffic hit the streets as I advanced against the grain. My pace sped up as my mind twirled like a Ferris wheel. *He was your son.*

Regret killed me and ripped my chest apart as I imagined a much younger version of myself stealing moments of physical pleasure. Every orgasm haunted me at that very second. *What if she's telling the truth?* Years of happiness with the most incredible woman on the planet could go up in smoke. Visions of Antoinette rushing into the concert hall to view MC ET's corpse intercepted my attention. *He was your son.*

I snapped out of my daydream and caught myself passing St. Rita High School. The truck coasted past a Mickey D's and I busted a right on 79th Street. With nobody to turn to, I thought about calling Greg. *He might be busy with his family.* So I headed in the direction of West Englewood, Chicago. Kyle resided in a one-bedroom apartment off 71st and Paulina.

He welcomed me into his home. By the time he handed me a second beer, I'd caught him up to speed on just about everything that went down since the concert. Next, I told him about the news Antoinette broke to me at the mall.

"She told you MC ET was your son?" Kyle almost went into shock, too. We kicked it in his dining room area on either side of a poker table. "Damn, man. That's has to be hard news to accept."

"Tell me about it. Don't know if I should believe her, or write her off as a Looney Tune." Common sense told me to walk away.

"Part of me hopes she never contacts me again. But the other part of me is curious. What if he was indeed my son?"

"I dunno, fam'." Kyle took a sip from his bottle. "What if she would've told you she was pregnant back in the day?"

My eyes opened wide, and I shook my head no. "That's hard to say, bro'. Back then? At that young age, I probably would've pushed her to get an abortion. 'Cause Colisa most likely would've left me and had the marriage annulled if she found out. My family wouldn't be where it is today."

"Okay, that's probably the same logic she used when she decided to keep her baby." He did his best to make me feel better and show that he understood. "I got mixed emotions, though. 'Cause if I had a son, I would want to know about him. Give me a chance to be that father figure."

"So you see where I'm comin' from." Too many questions filled the air. A huge part of me wanted the truth about Eric and his mother. "I wouldn't know where to start if I told my wife the full story about Antoinette. I'm tempted to try and get to the bottom of whatever's going on. Even without Doug."

Kyle sat his beer on the nearest coaster and leaned into the table. "You know I got ya' back, cuz. However you want to play it."

"I want to shed some light on the entire situation. If you're down with me, then let's find out who killed him." I didn't know how much of my motivation came from Eric Taylor possibly being my son. Maybe a good portion of it extended from me dusting off my second bottle of beer. Whatever the case, the moment for action rolled around. "But first, I need to check on my homie."

The host grabbed his coat and his keys. "I'll drive."

We hit the avenue and headed to St. Bernard Hospital to get an update on Doug. The temperature on the dashboard rested at forty-four degrees. The sun hit the horizon as we headed alongside people going home from work. The radio played the evening mix show on low volume. The DJ mashed up the a cappella version of Greg's verse to "Hip-Hop Villains" over the instrumental of "Steady Mobbin'" by Ice Cube.

My adrenaline escalated. I pumped it up louder, and we rolled along as if we had theme music.

Kyle waited in the hallway as I entered Doug's room. I greeted his family members and noticed the oxygen tube nowhere to be found. He rested on his back with his shoulder bandaged under a huge brace.

"He's been asking about you." His sister gave me the update as she stood beside his bed. "He came around earlier today."

He rested with his eyes closed. Wires still connected to multiple parts of his body. The heart monitor beeped away at a steady pace.

"Go ahead and talk to him for a moment. He's been relaxing well so far." She led the other family members out the door.

I moved to his bedside. It threw me to catch him in such a vulnerable position.

"I heard you totaled my car." His eyelids crept open, and he cracked a smile. "You owe me a new ghetto Batmobile."

I chuckled at his attempt at humor. His presence of mind to crack a joke pleased me. "I'm gonna get you on the chessboard when you get outta here."

"I haven't played chess in years." Doug's eyes drifted into space as he reminisced.

Reality kicked in after a few seconds of silence.

Doug closed his eyes. "That kid, Simone."

My heart sunk. "I know, man."

"I feel guilty for what happened," he said.

Guilt? You have no idea. I cut my eyes away from him and strolled to the window. "I feel you on that one."

"Have you talked to Antoinette?"

"Yes." The image of her crying before me at the mall popped

in my head. *He was your son.* "We need to get to the bottom of this situation. I'm gonna keep trying to find out who killed Eric."

One of the machines near Doug's bed beeped a little faster. "You sure you want to be out there after all that's happened? You were lucky, but look at me. Look at that kid."

"You're right, man." What he said made a lot of sense. I agreed, but I couldn't tell him about the new connection to Antoinette's drug. No words could be said yet about MC ET being my son. "But I want to find out who's behind all this."

"I don't want you to get hurt or killed, man. But I support you." Doug coughed a few times. "What's your next move?"

"Kyle's rollin' with me." I approached Doug's bed and paused by his side. "We're gonna cash in on a visit with our old friend, Goldie Gold."

The media pointed at Stallion Pee and the Gangster Disciples. However, Goldie Gold managed the victim's career, and they both rolled with the Vice Lords. He held the best odds on being able to shed some light on the situation. Kyle and I believed Eric's last message had everything to do with Antoinette's designer drug. We set out to seek answers.

Goldie Gold's building stood right off 51st and Ashland. Two residential apartments occupied the top floors of the three-story structure. A yellow sign with red and blue letters sat above the ground level door. It read *Gold Basket Food & Liquors.*

Kyle and I parked in the parking lot across the way. Streetlights lit up the night as we crossed the avenue. Two men in their early twenties smoked squares as they hung out in front of the store in winter coats. The door chimed as we entered.

"What's up, gentlemen?" David Simmons chilled behind the counter with his big eyes and round head. He recognized us right away and greeted us like a Vice Lord. "All is well ."

"It's all good, my dude." I responded in a way to neither uplift nor disrespect the gang slogan. "We tryna holla at Goldie."

"Hold fast." He looked us up and down. A frown came across his face as he pulled out his cell. He pressed a button, and then held it to his ear for a few seconds. "You got company."

Bottles of pint and half pint liquor were spread along shelves behind him. The side of the counter facing us housed gum, candy, and potato chips. I followed Kyle's eyes and caught a pistol on the lower shelf behind the counter.

"All is well. It's Inner City Youth." David chuckled into the phone as he kept it to his ear. He disconnected and pointed us to the back of the store. "Step right through."

We glided through the small store past the beer and canned goods. A door at the rear of the establishment led us to an office area. The cozy space housed a card table and a portable bar. Our old friend, Goldie Gold, sat behind a desk.

"You boys have been all over the TV lately." He leaned back in his chair and took an unlit cigar out his mouth. His other hand pointed at me. "And *you* walked away from a pretty rough accident."

"Yeah, I was lucky as I don't know what. I'm mad happy to be able to stand here today." We strolled toward the desk and posed behind two chairs that faced Goldie. I acknowledged his position in his organization. "We know you the man around these parts, and we hope you can help us."

"Have a seat, gentlemen." He gestured to the chairs as he sat the cigar in an empty ashtray. "What can I do for you?"

Kyle and I parked it beside each other. A computer monitor and a lamp sat between us and Goldie Gold.

"Well, we haven't had the chance to talk since the concert." *Where is this guy's head at?* I slumped forward and rubbed my hands together. "Your client was killed. That had to be a lot on you."

"Hell yeah, it's a lot. And he was much more than a client to me. You obviously have no clue about that." He frowned and leaned on the desk. "I'm definitely lookin' for the muthafucka that killed him."

Seems genuinely upset about it. I wanted to see how much he would share with us. "Everybody on TV has Stallion Pee convicted and ready to go to the chair. However, all the hard evidence points to the Vice Lords. That's *your* people."

Goldie Gold grimaced and pointed his finger in my direction as if he wanted to get angry. His mouth opened, but he caught himself. He relaxed in his seat and smiled. "You fellas are askin' a lotta interesting questions. Are y'all a Hip-Hop crew or an investigative branch of the federal government?"

Okay, this nigga's actin' funny. I rubbed my chin and peered into his eyes like he stole something.

Kyle glanced at me briefly. He cut his focus to Goldie. "We're just lookin' for some answers, dog. You might have some of the same questions yourself."

Goldie returned my stare for a second. He steered his attention to Kyle as he pointed to me with his thumb. "Ya' boy over here needs to be careful with his approach. Eric meant the world to me."

"If Eric meant that much to you, then you should be straight up with us." I peeked over at Kyle, and then directed my attention to Goldie. "All three of us go way back, so you can answer this question. Did you have anything to do with Eric's murder?"

Goldie Gold gazed at me like I was crazy. "There are two reasons why I'm not gonna fuck you up for asking me a question like that. Number one, we do indeed go way back. Number two, I realize his mother hired ya' boy to investigate, and you're taggin' along for the ride. So I'm only gonna say this one time. No, I had nothing to do with Eric's murder."

I respected his answer. My next question flowed off my tongue. "Do you know who shot at us and killed that kid?"

"No," he said, "but it probably was the same muthafuckas who cuffed the stash."

Cuffed the stash? My curiosity jumped off. *What's this nigga talkin' 'bout?* Kyle and I made eye contact.

"Don't tell me." Goldie squinted as his eyes cut between Kyle and me. "She didn't tell y'all about the stash."

I shrugged like a little kid. It didn't surprise me at all that there was more to add.

"Keep what I'm about to share on the low. I'm sure Antoinette's worried about losing her job." Goldie Gold rose from the desk and strolled to the office door. He twisted the latch and it locked. "She sells me drugs every once in a blue moon. Every so often, she gets her hands on some GSRA. It's important it goes to only certain clientele, so it won't get in the wrong hands. But this time, somebody snatched her stash before she could sell it to me."

"So her son took it." Kyle jumped in. He frowned and asked the obvious question. "He said something about that in his last message to the world, right?"

"That's the strange part," Goldie Gold spoke as he returned to his seat behind the desk. "As far as I know, Eric knew nothing about GSRA. That message confuses me, but I'm gonna get to the bottom of this."

"I feel the same way." *He was your son.* Antoinette's face appeared before me with tears shooting down her cheeks. "Old girl just told me today that I was his father."

Goldie frowned in confusion. "You were *whose* father?"

"Eric Taylor. She kept it from me for all these years and *just* told me," I said.

"No, that's bullshit!" Goldie Gold spoke confidently. "We went to the—"

The lamp snatched everyone's attention as it repeatedly strobed on and off.

Goldie clipped his sentence and focused on the computer screen. "Aw, okay. They must've let him out the county."

"What's the deal, yo'?" I asked. "Who?"

He sprung to his feet and spun the computer monitor to face us. Surveillance software divided the screen into four sections. The top areas showed two outside camera angles. The bottom sections displayed separate camera shots from inside the liquor store. Three male figures stood in front of the register.

I grew concerned.

Goldie Gold pointed to a brown-skinned man in a black skullcap. He stood in front of the counter and spoke to David Simmons. Goldie said, "That's the nigga I've been waiting to talk to, right there."

"Wait a minute." Kyle screwed up his face. "Is that MC ET's hype man?"

"Yeah. That fool has a lotta nerve showing up around here." Goldie pulled a Glock from the top drawer on the desk. A full clip followed, and he clicked it into place. The gun went to the rim of his pants in the back. "I have to ask you gentlemen to excuse me."

Kyle and I made eye contact. I shrugged my shoulders.

Goldie made sure his shirt covered the weapon as he passed us and exited the office. The door shut behind him. Kyle and I directed our attention to the computer monitor. He stomped into the liquor store and came face to face with MC ET's hype man and his crew. The camera angle gave us a clear view of the hype man's face and the back of Goldie's head. They exchanged greetings and casual mannerisms, at first. Soon, the conversation escalated, and we could hear them through the door.

"Look man, where is the money!" The hype man beat Goldie Gold to the draw and produced a gun. He aimed it at Goldie's forehead at point blank range.

Goldie's arms shot out to the side. The hype man's crew kept David Simmons covered.

I whispered to Kyle. "Damn, what's going on?"

His eyebrows shot to the sky. "I was about to ask *you*, cuz."

"I ain't playin' with you! Where is it?" The hype man grew

more aggressive. "Okay, I'm gone count to three. One . . ."

"Wait a minute! Slow down!" Goldie Gold pleaded. "Let's talk."

"The time for talking is over." He kept the pistol at his head. "Two . . ."

"Look, it ain't no money, man." Goldie's arms shook as if he didn't know what to do with them. "Calm down! Don't do anything stupid."

"Too late, nigga." The hype man arrived at the magic number. "Three!"

"Wait!" Goldie Gold reached behind his back for his pistol.

The hype man pulled the trigger.

POW!

Chapter Eighteen:
Goldie-Gold

The bottom left hand picture on the computer monitor displayed the angle from behind Goldie Gold's head. The bullet ripped through his skull. Blood, brains, and bones splattered against the camera lens. The frame blacked out. The other surveillance angle showed Goldie's body tilt backward headfirst. He collapsed to his back, lying motionless on the liquor store floor.

"No!" David Simmons yelled to the top of his voice.

"Shut the fuck up!" The hype man swung the gun around on David. "Stop cryin' like a bitch and tell us where the money is!"

David's eyes opened even wider than normal. His voice shook. "Man, I don't know about no money!"

The hype man rushed him and placed the gun to his head. "You'd better figure something out with the quickness, or else you can kiss the pavement with ya' boy over here!"

"I . . . I . . . I dunno," David pleaded with urgency. "For real. I wouldn't lie to you, man. I dunno!"

"Whatever, fool!" The hype man got more aggressive. "Show me the other room!"

Oh shit! My heart dropped. It dawned on me the maniac with the gun would head to the back of the store next. I grabbed Kyle's arm and pointed to the door behind the desk. "Over there."

"The other room is through the door," David answered the maniac. "Right there."

"Move it!" The gunman shooed David in our direction with his weapon. "Take me to the money!"

Kyle tipped to the closet and ducked inside. I darted into the bathroom and shut the door behind me. The lock bolted into place.

Click!

Darkness surrounded me except for the light shining beneath the door. I backed away and squatted to one knee against the wall.

The door to the office burst open.

The hype man's voice rang out. "Show me the money!"

"Man, I don't know about no money!" Fear came through David's voice.

"Don't fuckin' play with me!" The hype man spoke with bass and authority. "I ain't got no time to fuck around with you. You got five seconds. One . . ."

Thump, thump, thump!

My heart got the best of me.

"Aw shit, man!" The fear in David's voice changed to panic. "Goldie ain't neva' tell me nothin' 'bout no money!"

"Stop lyin', nigga. Two . . ."

"Come on, man!" David's voice cracked. "*Please* don't kill me. I ain't lyin' to you. It ain't nothin' I can tell you."

"You betta' make somethin' up then." The hype-man made his point and kept counting. "Three . . ."

My heart wouldn't stop its frenzied pace.

"Don't nobody give a fuck about you gettin' on yo' knees, fool! Four . . ."

The image of Goldie taking a bullet to the head crossed my

mind.

"I'll do anything, man! Don't shoot me!" Desperate shouts from David's mouth traveled through the bathroom door. "I don't want to die! Please!"

Sweat rolled down my face. I visualized David crouched over begging for his life. *Don't kill him. Oh, God!*

"Five!" The hype man reached the magic number. His pistol went off into the night. *POW!*

"Ugh!" David's voice shrieked. A one hundred-ninety pound thump vibrated the floor.

Everything went quiet.

"Damn, man. Why you shoot both of 'em?" One of his partners broke the silence with the voice of reason. "Now it ain't nobody to tell us where the dough is."

"I gave that nigga two extra seconds more than I normally give a nigga, and he still ain't say nothin'. Fuck 'im. The money's gotta be in this office somewhere." The hype man gave orders to his team. "Rip this place apart and find it."

Boxes and furniture rumbled around as shadows moved about under the door.

I froze, practically without breathing. *How am I gonna get outta here?*

The hype man directed his assistants. "You! Check the closet. You, check the bathroom."

Footsteps shuffled around outside. A shadow got larger under the door as one of the crooks approached. The doorknob rattled around for two seconds. "It's locked."

"Get out the way." One shadow moved to the left while another approached and paused.

POW! POW!

Two bullets ripped through the door and ricocheted around the bathroom.

I closed my eyes and covered my head. Every muscle in my

body clenched. I stilled myself to keep from making a sound.

The doorknob rattled again. "Shit, it's still locked. Stand back!"

POW! POW! POW!

More bullets bounced around the room.

No, I can't die like this! My forearms shielded my face as if they could stop bullets. I got down on both knees.

Somebody jiggled the doorknob. The hype man said, "It still ain't open!"

"Step to the side," the third partner's voice said. "Lemme take a shot at it."

Rat-tat-tat-tat-tat!

An automatic weapon sprayed the door.

What the . . . I closed my eyes and curled up in the corner as tight as I could. Bullets clattered the walls and shattered the mirror. The weapon stopped, and I glanced up. Light shined through more holes in the door. Somebody tried to open it, but it wouldn't budge.

"What the hell they make this lock out of? The money *must* be in there." The hype man's shadow covered the holes in the door as he peeped through. He stepped backward one pace. "I'm 'bout to kick this muthafucka down."

WHAM!

His foot slammed against the door. He paused for a moment, and his foot walloped into it again.

WHAM!

The hinges came loose.

Oh shit! Panic kicked in. A killer with a deadly weapon stood seconds away from finding me.

"Wait, hold up!" The first sidekick got everyone's attention. "It's over here . . . I found it!"

Footsteps scuffled around as all the shadows progressed to one side. Boxes bumbled.

"Oh yeah, baby! Jackpot!" The hype man got excited. "Put it all in this sack."

I inhaled and exhaled in slow motion. My body never moved from the curled up position. From the sounds of things, Kyle should've been okay.

"All is well with the drugs. All is well with this part of the cheese. One more bag of dough to grab tonight." The hype man's voice escalated. "First thing in the mornin' we'll be ready to get outta town."

One of the sidekick's voices stopped the flow. "Let me get my cut now."

"Look, this *ain't* the time to be petty." The hype man got angry. "It's time for business. Don't start!"

A second sidekick came out of nowhere. "The plan? Want me to do the plan now?"

"What plan?" the first sidekick replied.

"Everyone just relax for now. There's more work to do." The hype man took charge of his workers. "Let's bounce, pick up these flunkies, and hit the next spot."

Footsteps shook the floor as they mumbled among themselves. The shadows under the door and through the bullet holes motioned from right to left. A few seconds later, silence took over. One could hear a pin drop except for the heating system that purred like a kitten.

I moved from my curled up position and came to one knee. The bullet holes worked as peepholes for me.

Papers lay scattered around the office. Furniture turned over. Boxes of miscellaneous debris appeared in every direction. David Simmons' body rested on the floor in the middle of it all.

The lock on the door twisted in slow motion. I tipped out and noticed the puddle of blood beneath David. The surveillance cameras showed the liquor store empty and nobody around outside. Careful not to step in any blood, I made my way to the closet and knocked softly.

I whispered, "Kyle?"

He opened the door and got a load of the scene. "Aw shit."

We soaked it all in for about ten seconds.

Reality hit, and I didn't want to be around another crime scene investigation. "Let's get outta here."

We stepped around David's body and hustled through the office door into the liquor store. Goldie Gold's corpse lay spread eagle in a puddle of blood and brains of its own. We hopped over and around him and trotted toward the front door.

"Wait a minute." Kyle paused and ducked behind the register. "I saw Dave write something down as Goldie stepped out the back office."

My curiosity jumped off. I stopped in my tracks to see if Kyle had anything.

"It's an address and a name." He grabbed a receipt and read a location off the back written in ink. "Houston. 206 South Jefferson Street."

"Doesn't ring a bell." I scanned the store for the last time. "Let's go, dog."

We ducked across the street and broamed off in Kyle's ride. My mind went crazy about everything going on. The sunset crept up on us as we rolled along in stunned silence. The hype man's words echoed in my head. *All is well with the drugs. All is well with this part of the cheese. One more bag of dough to grab tonight.*

"You thinking what I'm thinking?" Kyle asked as he pulled up and stopped at a light. "The hype man has got to be the one we're after. Sounded like they're plannin' to rob somebody else."

"I'm comin' to the same conclusion." I knew nothing about the money the hype man sought. But I would be willing to bet the drugs he spoke of came from Antoinette. "But why would he shoot MC ET? I thought that was his boy?"

"That's a good question." Kyle busted a left onto Ashland Avenue. "I could tell David wrote the address on the back of this receipt to send a message. Maybe it's the address to the next place they plan to hit. This location might mean something."

A huge part of me wanted to check it out. No lead beat the one before us. The hype man's voice smashed me in the head. *First thing in the mornin' we'll be ready to get outta town.* The clock ticked. *Once the morning hits, it may be too late to do anything.* Everything leaned in the direction of going to check out that address.

My wife's voice drubbed me. *Just remember who'll be hurt if something really happens to you.* Thoughts of Linda and Dorian popped to the forefront of my mind. *Maybe I should just tell everything to Detective Timms.* "The address may indeed be a spot that needs to be checked out, but I don't know if we should be the ones to roll to it."

"You sure, bro'? I know you still got a lotta unanswered questions." He switched lanes and passed a car. "I don't know if you still keep a shotgun at the crib, but I do. Whatever you want to do, you know I got ya' back."

My marbles bounced around, and they all landed on Goldie Gold's words after I mentioned my paternal relation to Eric. *No, that's bullshit. We went to—* I wanted to go to Antoinette's place to get real answers. But an even larger part of me didn't want to see her at all.

I took a deep breath and made my decision. "Take me to my ride."

"To your truck?" Kyle's eyebrows crumpled with confusion. "You going home to grab your gun?"

"No." My mind took off in a different direction. "There's something I have to do."

"All right, homie." He drove in silence for ten seconds, and then asked, "Are you sure, man?"

"Positive." I focused my mind on my destination.

"What about the cops?" He asked a logical question. "They're gonna come searching for us as soon as they see the surveillance tape."

"You're right." I thought about it for a moment. "When they come through on you, just tell them the truth. We ain't got nothin' to hide when it comes down to it."

We arrived at Kyle's crib, and he dropped me off. I hopped in my vehicle and sat there for a few moments. It warmed up as I debated with myself on which course of action to take. I took off and made my way across the Southside. After driving for a while, I ended up at Antoinette's place.

I parked down a few houses and across the street. A news truck with a fifty-foot antennae extended to the sky sat near her building. A reporter stood tall on the sidewalk with her back to Antoinette's doorway. She posed with her microphone and spoke into a camera. Stream rose from her mouth with every word she uttered.

The reporter took a small break that lasted about five minutes. The truck engine hummed as it kept me warm. The cameraman shot at her again as she spoke. Two minutes later, they wrapped it up. The antennae descended into the van, and they took off into the night. I watched Antoinette's place for another twenty minutes. As much as I wanted to bang on her door and question her, I didn't. *Nothing good can come from me being here.* Questions, answers, and lies needed to be sorted. But I couldn't trust the woman behind those doors, so I shifted my ride into drive and pulled away.

My mind wandered as I cruised the Chicago night. Several moments passed before I pulled up in my driveway. The garage door went up, and I noticed Colisa's parking space empty. *She must still be at her mother's.* The door descended, and I tossed my coat over a dining room chair. I skipped up the stairs and heard video games coming from Dorian's room. My bedroom door shut behind me. I flopped on the bed.

He was your son. Antoinette's voice wouldn't go away. I sat there not knowing what to do. The clock ticked and ticked. I chilled and waited for five-O to ring my doorbell. *He was your son.* Eric Taylor remained in the forefront of my mind. I couldn't let his hype man get away. Using the house phone, I dialed Detective Timms' number. I intended to tell him everything. However, the call went straight to voicemail. I planned to leave the detective a message, but I hung up. *That young man could've indeed been my son.*

I came to my feet as I made my next call.

Kyle answered on the other end.

"I'm 'bout to come scoop you," I said. "Let's go check out that address and see if we can find this fool."

Chapter Nineteen:
The Hype Man

Kyle and I conversed briefly and disconnected the call. I snatched open the bedroom door to find my nephew standing there. He caught me off guard. I said, "Dorian?"

"It's me in the flesh, Uncle Dre." He had a little bass in his voice this time. His chest poked out, and he held his chin up. "I know it's more going on than you tell me, but I want to help. Can I roll?"

I froze in my tracks for a second. My little nephew was on manhood's front door. He would've been well into adulthood in some cultures. And he looked just like my little sister. I set the phone down. "Sorry, kid."

"C'mon, Uncle Dre." He frowned and stuck his palms toward the sky. "I can handle myself."

The visual of Simone drowning in his own blood in my arms hit my mind. I stomped past Dorian and ducked into the bathroom. "It's too dangerous, son. I'm not gonna lose you like I lost that young man the other night."

"I'm tired of being treated like a kid." He followed me and stood in the bathroom door. "Take me with you. I won't tell Aunt Lisa."

"I know you won't 'cause you ain't goin'." I wet my face towel and blotted it across my grill. "Stop trippin' like I'm goin' to Great America without you. This is dangerous business."

"Dag, I can't do nothin'." He pouted and stormed away.

Be mad if you wanna. I ain't gonna lose another son. Mouthwash swished around in my mouth for a few. I spat into the sink and then stared into the mirror. *Let's do this.*

I hit the basement and grabbed my shotgun from the top shelf of the back room and swiped ammunition from the cabinet. No way would I let old boy get away with killing MC ET and Goldie Gold. I came up the stairs and placed the gun in the backseat. The Blazer rolled to West Englewood.

Kyle trotted down his front stairs carrying a paintball gun case. Per our conversation, I knew he packed a sawed-off shotgun. He placed his heat in the back.

"I got some information about MC ET's hype man." Kyle slammed the car door and strapped himself in. "Him and ET grew up together. His name is Paul Adams."

"How'd you find that out?" I guided the ride down the road and adjusted the heat.

"Off the Internet." He used a matter of fact tone. "He dropped out of Simeon four years ago. Spent a couple weekends here and there in jail for possession. He also had a car theft they reduced to joyriding. They questioned him the night of the murders and kept him on a traffic warrant. He got out the county earlier today."

"We heard him say they're planning to leave town in the morning." I merged the truck onto the expressway. "This may be the last chance for anyone to catch 'im."

He pointed to the road ahead. "It's on, man."

"Blue Sky" by Common thumped through the speakers. We headed to the downtown area to explore the address. Traffic flowed nonstop as the clock approached midnight. The digital dashboard read forty-one degrees. As soon as the Dan Ryan changed into the

Kennedy, we exited at Jackson Street. The west view of the skyline towered over us as we broamed to the corner of Jefferson and Adams.

We pulled up to a huge warehouse looking tower. I parked across the street, and we gazed up at a six-story structure. Each window appeared dark from the outside.

Not knowing where to start, I stated the obvious. "This is a big-ass building."

"Yeah, I wonder what we're looking for." Kyle snatched his bag out the back. "There's a lotta ground to cover. Do we go inside? Is there something outside the place?"

"This is like a stab in the dark." I climbed out the car and opened the back door to get to my gun. "What if we don't find anything?"

"There's a chance that might happen." He posed with his weapon in his hand. Kyle tossed the carrying sack into the backseat. "But dude looked like he wanted someone to see this address. Hopefully, we find the hype man."

We covered our guns the best we could with our coats and crossed the street. The doors at the main entrance did not open.

"You check things out that way." I pointed one way while I moved in the opposite direction. "I'll see what I can find over here."

We separated, and I trotted to the end of the building. I peeped around the corner and laid eyes upon a passageway. Step by step, I checked out the structure. *Nothin' to write home about.* I got to the end of the building and saw Kyle at the far corner. We met in the middle in front of a loading dock. Two huge openings created driveways where trucks could back in. We checked out opposite driveways and snooped around. Kyle went up a flight of stairs along the wall and found something first.

"Yo, check this out," he whispered loud as hell to get my attention. His hand pressed against a door that gave way. "I found a way in."

I jogged to his side. We peeped in as he held the door that led to the inside of the loading area. Brown boxes were stacked tall against the far wall. We tipped in holding shotguns, looking like two ghetto Elmer Fudds hunting 'wabbits' and shit. A door across the area led to a stairway. Both of us entered and paused once inside.

"Let's split up." I glanced down the hall to see several doors on opposite sides of the corridor. "You take the even floors, and I'll start with this one. We'll meet at the top."

Kyle disappeared up the stairs. I slid into the first floor hallway. Six doors appeared in front of me, three on each side. As I stepped through the dark hall, I observed my surroundings. I twisted the doorknob on the first two doors, and they didn't budge. Each pace echoed against the walls as I strolled along the way. The next door on the right didn't open. But the one across from it did.

I peeked into an area with a small table against the wall and a refrigerator. A sink completed what appeared to be a break room. I scanned around to find a pop machine and nothing to note. None of the other doors along the first floor opened.

I busted through a door at the end of the hall and climbed a stairway to the second floor. Kyle came out a door on that floor and met me there.

"What you find?" I asked.

"Not too much." He unzipped his coat with one hand as he carried his gun with the other. "An empty hallway and a bunch of locked doors."

"Same here." I climbed the stairs ahead of him. "You sure it was 206 South Jefferson Street?"

He followed and flashed a piece of paper from his pocket. "Yeah, I got the receipt right here."

I glanced at the original handwriting in ink from the liquor store. It dawned on me that nobody knew of our actions at that moment. We had no backup, and we couldn't hide behind Doug's private eye shield. Nobody would know where to look if we got hurt or killed. *I guess someone would eventually stumble across my car.* Butterflies kicked in. I ducked into the door leading to the third floor. Kyle shot up another flight.

The exit signs on either end of the hallway acted as nightlights. Along with the soft lamps on the walls, it provided just enough light to barely see. I stepped down the way, glancing over my shoulders every two paces. The knobs on the first two doors didn't budge when I attempted to twist them. I arrived at the third door and read the sign on the wall beside it to myself. *Houston.*

The door gave way without me having to barely touch it. It creaked open as wide as it would go. The illumination from the hall revealed office space divided into two cubicles. Computer monitors were positioned on opposite corners on one side of the room. Each desk had a phone and a stapler, along with miscellaneous office supplies. No personal pictures or nametags.

The door shut behind me. Total darkness took over except for the lights from the phones and the fax machine. I turned and caught another sparkle of light toward the bottom of a door at the back of the office. I gripped my shotgun and advanced to the entryway. The doorknob turned. The next room extended twice the length of the first office space. A soft light from a bathroom at the far end provided some light. Three tables sat in the middle of the floor. Four professional level printers were scattered about the room. A dorm room sized refrigerator rested in the corner near an old school floor model printer. On the right, fold up card tables and chairs were stacked way in the rear.

I stepped through an entrance that led me to the office space next door. More tables and chairs were stacked to the ceiling. I explored further, and a path between the chairs and tables led to another door at the end of the room. It also connected the two offices. The bathroom and the first stack of chairs and tables appeared before me. I glanced over the entire space from the rear. It resembled a miniature version of Kinko's attached to an empty office somebody used as storage space.

Click.

The light in the front office popped on.

Confusion set in. My eyebrows came together.

"This door was unlocked, too. Just like they said. Let's get this money and get outta here." The hype man stormed into the office. He gripped his pistol with leather gloves. "The safe is behind a floor model printer."

Oh shit! I glanced at my surroundings and squatted to the ground.

"There should be two desks in the first room." His sidekick busted through the door wearing black and silver baseball gloves and carrying an automatic rifle. "And the fridge and the printer supposed to be in the second."

I got a good view of them through the stack of chairs. They searched around the area.

A third partner followed wearing nighttime shades and gripping a Glock handgun. He also wore gloves. "Y'all find it?"

"Yeah. It's back here." The hype man raised his voice, so his partners could hear. He slid the printer out the way and a safe appeared mounted into the wall. "Where them fools at with the combination?"

"They're comin'." Old boy with the shades kept watch at the front door. "I see 'em in the hall."

Thump, thump, thump!

I found myself in a tight space with the killer a few feet away from me, again. *Deja vu than a muthafucka.*

"I want my cut as soon as we see it," old boy with the shades said.

"I done told you. Don't start!" the hype man replied.

The younger one in the black and silver gloves directed his attention to the hype man. "Do the plan now?"

"No, not yet." The hype man glanced at his watch. "Where these fools at?"

"What plan y'all keep talkin' 'bout?" Old boy with the shades got angry. "That's why I don't trust y'all."

"This is not the time or the place for this." The hype man grimaced and grit his teeth. "I ain't gone say it no more!"

Two more peeps entered the room. They sparked my memory right away. *That's old boy from the house party and his partner.* The man in the red coat that threatened to kill Doug, Simone, and me stood a few feet away from the hype man.

"My people said they would leave the combination behind the pop machine in the first floor break room." He rocked his red baseball cap to the back in the wintertime. His bare fingers clinched a folded piece of paper. "It was exactly where it was supposed to be."

"Hurry up and open this bitch." The hype man slid the printer to the side some more to make room. He pointed to the front and spoke to the first two thugs. "Y'all keep an eye on the door and hold down the hallway."

They stared each other down for five seconds, and then parted ways. Old boy with the shades exited into the hallway, while the one with the rifle secured the entrance to the office. The dude from the house party adjusted his baseball cap and squatted to the level of the safe. He glanced at the paper in one hand and manipulated the knob with the fingers of his other. The hype man hung over his shoulder.

Sweat collected under my armpits like crazy. It ran down my forehead as well. I really wanted to take off my coat, but I didn't budge or make a sound. The base of the shotgun rested on the ground. My hands gripped the barrel.

"Got it!" Dude twisted the latch, and the safe pealed open. His eyes bucked as he stared inside. "There it is!"

The hype man shoved dude in the red cap out the way. He froze and spread his arms like he wanted to hug the safe. "Cash money, just like I like. This is what I'm talkin' 'bout. Y'all two fill up that bag."

The hype man took a couple steps back and gave them room. They stumbled to the safe. Dude in the red cap held a black duffle bag open while his partner swiped stacks of cash into it with his naked palms. Dude struggled to press the opening of the bag together while his partner zipped it tight. They both came to a full stand before the hype man. His back faced me through the folded chairs.

I wanted to pull some type of super-cop move and overpower them all. However, reality kept me still. Sweat rolled down my chest like a waterfall.

"Go sit the cash by the front door." The hype man pointed toward the entrance.

Dude's partner secured the Velcro around the handles and scooped up the bag. He trotted past the cubicles and set it near the guy with the rifle.

Dude in the red cap titled his head to the hype man. "We got the dough, fam'."

"Yeah, good job," he replied. "Too bad it's your last one."

"My last one?" Dude frowned in confusion. "Why?"

"'Cause your time is up . . . fam'." The hype man aimed his gun at the dude in the red cap and pulled the trigger.

POW! POW!

I jumped out my skin and stood up a little.

One bullet penetrated dude's skull and flew out the rear of his head. The other ripped through his torso. He came off his feet and sailed backward. His body slammed into the printer. Arms flew out to his sides and he slithered to the ground.

Dude's partner sprinted in our direction and stopped in his

tracks. His mouth dropped to the ground. Hands shot out to his sides as he frowned in confusion. "What the fuck, man?"

Blood streaked down the side of the printer. Dude's brains sprayed across the wall and the ceiling.

My heart rate picked up. I panted heavily like a canine.

"Time's up, man." The hype man swung the gun around on old boy's partner. "It's been real."

He felt around his waist in vain. "This is why we couldn't bring our guns."

"Yep," the hype man agreed as his trigger finger went to work. *POW! POW! POW!*

Bullets exploded through dude's partner's body and forehead. He staggered backward three steps and caught himself from falling. His fists clenched and he strained every muscle in his body to remain standing. Blood rolled down his face as he flopped to one knee. He huffed and puffed and pointed a finger at the hype man. Blood bubbled in his mouth as he spoke. "Fuck you, Paul! I'll see you in hell!"

POW!

The hype man put a final bullet in old boy's head.

He collapsed forward. His face slapped the floor and blood puddled around his corpse.

My mouth dropped wide open. I held my palm over it in disbelief as my body shook in terror.

Old boy with the automatic weapon shoved the duffle bag to the side with his foot. He strolled to the back and addressed the hype man. "You done with them niggas?"

"Yeah." The hype man swung his gun back and forward between the bodies as if he wasn't sure they were dead. "We definitely don't need these clowns anymore."

"Ain't nobody else's prints on this AK but his." Old boy dropped the automatic weapon on dude's partner. He did an about face and returned to the front of the office. "Let's hurry up and get outta here, man."

The hype man tossed his gun on top of dude with the red cap. He put forth extra effort not to step in any blood.

I held my position. *Looks like they're about to bounce.* A slight sense of relief came over me. I wondered if the guns they left behind were the same ones used to kill MC ET and Simone. I couldn't wait to tell the cops what I'd seen. *Those have got to be the murder weapons.* My eyes remained focused on the hype man as he moved about.

CLICK!

The sound of a Glock being locked and loaded rang off inches away from my ear.

My nerves jittered, and my eyes bucked as wide as they could go. While maintaining my squatting position, I slowly rotated around on my toes.

The thug in the nighttime shades towered over me. He frowned and aimed his pistol at my head. "You're a *dead* man!"

Chapter Twenty:
Headlights

I cast my eyes up at a gun in position to blow me into Kingdom Come. The barrel aimed at me at point blank range.

"Stand yo' punk ass up!" Nighttime Shades guided me to my feet with his pistol.

"What? It's somebody back there?" Hype Man's voice went up two octaves. He squinted and frowned as he took a step in my direction. "Who the hell is that?"

"It's that nigga from the news." Shades shoved me with his free hand. "The old cat that crashed his car into that truck."

I stumbled around the stacked up tables and chairs. My shotgun remained on the floor.

"Dr. Dre?" Hype Man grew more angry and confused. "What the hell you doin' here?"

My heart throbbed out of control. I sensed major tension from the gun at the back of my head. *Lie to these niggas.* I stuck out my chest. "I'm here to rob this muthafucka, too."

Hype Man raised his voice. "Shut yo' lyin' ass up!"

Old boy with the shades slugged me in the back of my neck

with his pistol.

WHAM!

"Oh!" Pain rushed from the rear of my head through the front. I whirled one hundred eighty degrees as my body collapsed to the floor.

Nighttime Shades skyscraped over me and aimed his Glock between my eyes. "I should put yo' ass to sleep!"

"No! Not here." Wrinkles embedded themselves in the hype man's face. His eyeballs burned a hole through me. "Nigga, you fuckin' up a perfect crime."

Dude with the black and silver gloves posed on the other side of the bodies. "What we gone do with him?"

"Bring 'im with us. Tonight, we sink his ass to the bottom of Lake Michigan." Hype Man stepped over me and snatched up my shotgun. "For now, let's get outta here."

Excruciating soreness bombarded my skull as I lay there. I huffed and puffed as I slowly blinked and tried to focus.

"Get up, fool!" Nighttime Shades cocked back his foot. His leg swung forward, and his toes booted me in the gut.

"Umph!" Agony jolted me. I crunched up along the floor in a ball as I moaned in anguish.

"Ain't gone say it no more." He got voice strong with me. "Get up!"

My gut wrenched in knots like I had to shit.

Four images of the man with the sunglasses on at night rotated counterclockwise before me. The barrel of a black Tech Nine took the forefront in each frame of the kaleidoscope. I squinted and came to rest on all fours.

"This fool thinks I'm playin." He pressed the gun against my head. "I'm gone count to three. One . . ."

Oh shit! I lifted my head. Using both hands and five toes, I thrust myself up to a full standing position. The abrupt movement caused me to grow light-headed. My stomach bubbled, and I threw up at Nighttime Shade's feet.

He skipped backward four steps as he kept the gun on me. The frown on his face grew more intense. "You nasty nigga!"

I spit a few times and wiped my mouth as my view transformed from four images into one. Both victims' blood merged along the floor into an enormous puddle. It trapped Hype Man, Shades, and me at the rear of the print shop.

"Bring yo' ass this way." Shades snatched me by my arm and dragged me toward him. He kept the gun on me. "We can get out over here."

I skipped over the vomit and stumbled alongside him. The three of us trotted through the connecting store to the front. We passed by the first door that bridged the neighboring stores. Red Baseball Cap and his partner rested in enough blood to overflow a kiddie pool.

Hype Man unfastened the door. We galloped down the hallway. The back of my head thumped with each step. Nighttime Shades kept near me with the pistol as we cut around a corner into a freight elevator. Dude with the black and silver gloves waited for us to board with the duffle bag on the floor beside him. He shut the gate and hit the down switch. We descended in slow motion.

"I didn't want to have to kill you." The hype man spoke down to me like he was the judge and jury deciding my fate. "But you keep meddling around lookin' for trouble."

The elevator came to a stop on the first floor. Black and Silver unlatched the gate and let us out.

"Those flunkies had that other kid in check. But you butted in when you should've just stayed away. I heard you tried to get 'im to drop a dime on me." Hype Man led the way out the elevator to the loading area. "I got the message out to them from inside The County. They had the go ahead to put that dude to sleep if he even looked like he wanted to say anything about what he saw that night."

You gave the order to kill Simone? Rage kicked in. I trailed along as the gun aimed at my head.

They led me through the same door we used to enter the building. A white Chevy Express van with no windows sat parked on the street beside the driveway. The exit door slammed and clinked behind us.

Nighttime Shades tugged at it. "It's locked."

We climbed down the stairs along the wall to the floor of the garage. Shades kept the gun on me as we stepped toward the van. The hype man handed my shotgun to Black and Silver.

Headlights faded in from the left.

Everyone froze.

Hype Man slashed his hand through the air and whispered loud as hell, "Get down!"

Nighttime Shades shifted the gun and aimed it at me from above my head. I caught the hint and squatted with the others. He guided me across the garage. I waddled along like a duck and followed them up the stairs. We came to our feet and pressed our backs against the wall.

The brightness glared into the night and got larger as it drew near. A car motor rumbled louder and stronger as it approached. The vehicle slowed down and came to a stop in the street just before it hit our view. The headlights shined across the opening of the garage and blared on the back of the van.

Black and Silver made eye contact with the hype man. Hype Man rotated his neck and glanced past me at Shades. Nighttime Shades placed his eyes on me as he kept the gun in my face. His hand shivered.

This fool is nervous. I got a load of my surroundings and brought myself off the wall.

Nighttime Shades' eyes opened wide with confusion.

I raised one eyebrow and stared daggers into him. "What you gone do, nigga? Shoot me with five-O right there?"

"Umph!" A sharp pain crashed into my ribs from the back. My torso caved in and bent in a direction it wasn't mean to go. I cuffed my elbow and forearm into it. *Goddamn it!* I wanted to collapse to the ground, but I caught myself. I glanced around at the man who sucker punched me.

The hype man pulled his fist back. "Shut yo' ass up!"

Shades closed in on the other side of me. The barrel of the gun smashed against my ear. "Do that shit again, fool, and you die right now."

The headlights beamed bright and steady with no movement.

Please let this be five-O. Steam escaped from my mouth as I huffed and puffed. The affliction in the hindmost section of my dome convulsed. My rib cage twinged.

The headlights jerked, and the car drove forward. A blue, old school Cadillac pulled into view. It disappeared around the other side of the van.

Shit! Shock turned into fear. *What these boneheads gone do to me?*

"You stupid fool!" A grimy frown took over the hype man's face. His eyeballs ate me alive as he spoke about me in third person to his crew. "Get his ass to the van, so we can say good night!"

Shades shoved me with his freehand, and I stumbled forward. Black and Silver carried my shotgun and the duffle bag full of money. Hype Man glanced around as we stepped outside the garage. We double timed it to the van and gathered around the rear. The hype man keyed the door on the left and opened it.

"Put the dough and his gun in the back," he said, "then tie his ass up."

My heart rate sped up. *What am I gonna do?*

Black and Silver shoved the duffle bag in the van. He climbed in with my registered weapon. His footsteps bumbled around. He yelled out, "Don't see the plasticuffs!"

"Hurry up!" Hype Man vanished around the driver side. His

voice traveled over the vehicle. "This chump gone be sleepin' with the fishes in less than an hour."

Nighttime Shades' attention wandered away from me. He strolled to the van and ducked his head in the door behind Black and Silver. "Check in that bag right there."

I realized nobody had an eye on me. *This might be my chance to escape.* I tipped backward three steps, pivoted away from them, and blasted off like a rocket.

"Hey!" Nighttime Shades' voice traveled over my shoulder.

POW! POW!

His gun went off.

Bullets echoed into the night as they deflected off nearby objects. I lowered and covered my head as I sprinted across the street.

"No!" The hype man's voice traveled behind me. "Don't shoot 'im out here. Just catch his ass!"

I raced between two buildings as fast as I could. Each pace echoed off the brick structures. I didn't look back.

Multiple footsteps hit the pavement behind me. Their steps grew aggressive, and it felt like they wouldn't stop.

I darted through an alley and dashed past the next building. Black and Silver bolted out a gangway and cut me off at the past. He leaped off both feet and dived at my mid-section. I kept my stride and extended my palm to his face. My stiff-arm froze him in midair. His arms grabbed at me and slid from my waist to my ankles. He hit the pavement, but held a grip on my foot.

I tripped and stumbled forward. My face slammed to the concrete. We both skidded across the ground an additional ten feet. He came to his knees and tried to climb up to fully capture me. I drew back my leg and jolted a foot to his face.

WHAM!

His progress came to a halt, and his body collapsed as if he crashed into a brick wall.

In one motion, I crawled to my knees and scampered to my feet.

Nighttime Shades dived over Black and Silver and grabbed for me with both hands.

I weaved to one side. Shades sailed in the air and missed me completely. He crashed to the ground chest first. The hype man swung around to cut me off. I stopped in my tracks and broke in the opposite direction as I felt my wind catching up with me. He closed in on me and snatched a hold of my coat with both hands. I slowed down and tugged away, using my arm to chop across his. He struggled to catch his breath, too, but didn't let go. I braced myself on my next step and socked old boy across his face with a right.

WHAM!

His head jerked to the side, but he held on. He wrapped his arms around my waist and stumbled forward to tackle me.

We crashed to the concrete. Extreme exhaustion kicked in. I wrestled him off me the best I could. He grasped on to me tight. Nighttime Shades sized me up as he trotted toward me. He cocked back and dropped a right bomb across my chin.

My jaw shifted to one side.

Black and Silver approached me like Kevin Butler and booted me in the ribs.

"Oh!" My cry fizzled to the sky.

They pounded me with their fists and stomped me into the pavement. I tasted blood as I absorbed a beating that took me past the point of being able to defend myself. No parts of my face and torso went untouched. They whipped my ass.

Everything went dark.

Chapter Twenty-one:
Captured

My eyelids blinked a few times as they slowly crept open. The worst headache of my life snatched my attention. It banged and banged. My vision blurred. The view gradually came into focus as my eyes blinked a few more times. I found myself in the rearmost part of a van, resting on the floor on my backside.

The vehicle hit a bump. My body lifted in the air several inches and slammed to the black surface. Soreness snarled at my entire frame as I exhaled and moaned in agony.

"The dead has arisen." The hype man sat on a cushioned bench seat built into the wall. Sarcasm escaped his mouth. "Sorry we had to fuck you up like that."

I raised my hand to rub my face and realized my other arm moved along with it. They bound my wrists together with the same plasticuffs the police used for riot control. Further observance showed my ankles linked together as well.

"You should've left well enough alone, old timer." The hype man removed his hat. Dusty brown curly hair revealed itself in the form of a short fro. "'Hip-Hop Villains' was a little before my time, but I still liked y'all."

The van hit another bump and flopped me around. *This trap needs new shocks.* Hurt and discomfort could not be avoided while on my back. I lifted my head from the floor. My elbow pressed against the surface and boosted me until I sat upright.

Nighttime Shades rode in the front passenger seat. *Brown-skinned with thick eyebrows.* Black and Silver drove the van. *Brown-skinned with a goatee.* The only view of the outside came from the front windows. We rolled into the night down an expressway surrounded by farmland.

I wiped blood from the corner of my mouth as I glanced at the hype man. "Where y'all takin' me?"

"That don't matter. But you should be sayin' yo' prayers right about now." Three black duffle bags sat on the bench next to the hype man. He grabbed a gun out the one closest to him. "Talk to God, Jesus, Allah, Buddha, or whoever you need to talk to. You'll be meeting them all within the next thirty minutes."

Thump, thump, thump!

Colisa, Linda, and Dorian popped to the forefront of my mind. My wife's voice echoed in my head. *Just remember who'll be hurt if something really happens to you.* I did not realize my life would end so early.

Hype Man pulled out a red bandana and cleaned his weapon. Black and Silver kept his eyes on the road, and Nighttime Shades looked like he wanted to doze off.

Every area on my body throbbed from the beat down. I positioned myself as comfortably as I could. Curiosity popped off in my head. So I asked the question that the opportunity presented. *Call him by his name.* "Tell me, Paul. Why'd you kill Eric?"

"That's what I call a lotta nerve. You're about to die, and you're still poking around being nosey. Plus, you think we're on a first name basis now. That's crazy, but I like you. So I guess it won't hurt to answer." He paused and stared at me. "We took some girls to his house when his moms wasn't there. He went in his room with his chick and shut the door. After I put my freak to sleep on the couch, I fumbled around his house and came across a mother lode of GSRA."

Goldie Gold's response when I asked him who killed Eric popped in my mind. *It probably was the same muthafuckas who cuffed the stash.* I frowned and gave the hype man my full attention.

"I snuck it to the crib and hid it in a safe place. At the concert, I let MC ET know I had it. But I didn't let 'im know where I got it. He'd never even heard of it." Hype Man took his eyes off me and polished his gun. "When we came back in the building to get ready for our set, this clown sends a message to the world, letting everyone know we had a top secret government drug in our possession. I'd warned him dozens and dozens of times about puttin' our business out there on the Internet usin' that phone. This time, I snapped."

"Damn." I didn't want him to stop letting me in on the story. "What you do?"

"I pulled out my piece and blew him away. The bad part is I missed with the first couple shots. One of the bullets traveled to the stage and caught DJ Roscoe." The hype man actually showed a bit of remorse on his face. "I finished MC ET off in a moment of rage and jetted out the door. Y'all chased me and forced me to blow away one of the security guards."

This is all about Antoinette's designer drug. Fury burned inside of me. *She put Doug and me in harm's way over some dope. Now I'm 'bout to die over it.*

"We put Molotov cocktails around the perimeter of places when we may face danger," he explained. "You chased me right into the setup, and I had no choice but to defend myself. I wasn't even tyna kill you back then. Just keep you off me."

Whatever. My wheels turned as I examined the van to come up with an escape plan. I noticed my shotgun in a storage compartment under the bench the hype man sat on. *This must be some handyman's van.* I planted my feet flat on the floor as I leaned back on the wall. The plasticuffs damn near cut off the circulation to my hands.

"The police had me in custody." Hype Man stared down at me. "I just knew I was in jail for good. But they never accused me of killing MC ET. The time on that punk ass traffic warrant ran out. I'm out, and I'm *not* goin' back in."

We rolled up the expressway for another fifteen minutes or so. Black and Silver pulled off the freeway and busted a right down a dark road. I bounced and flopped around until we arrived at our destination. The van stopped on an upward slope. I only saw the cloudy nighttime sky from where I sat.

The hype man gripped his pistol as he stared at me. "It's time."

Over a million butterflies danced around from my throat, to my stomach, and again to my throat. The back of the van opened. Black and Silver held onto the door as Shades stood a few feet back with his pistol on me.

"Go on." The hype man nodded at the door. "Get out."

I rolled over on my elbow and scooted my butt to the edge of the van. A gust of frigid air whooshed in on me. I swung my feet around; they dangled above the ground. Inch by inch, I moved up and managed to keep my balance as I exited the van.

I landed on the cracked pavement of an old parking lot. It connected to an abandoned forest preserve. Latin King graffiti displayed on a boarded up field house about thirty yards away.

"This way." Nighttime Shades guided me across a bunch of gravel that used to be grass. He kept the gun and his eyes on me as he strolled sideways. "Don't try anything stupid."

"I don't know what you expect me to try and do," I said as I hopped along with my ankles together. My muscles throbbed. I huffed and puffed from exerting so much energy. "I can't keep up."

"Keep it movin'," the hype man ordered.

I tried to do what he said, but I had no more power. My knees wobbled like spaghetti, and I spilled to the ground.

"Get up!" Hype Man yelled.

Shades kept me covered with the Glock. Black and Silver stood behind him.

"You got two choices." The hype man shoved me with his foot. "You can get yo' ass up and hop over to this ledge. Or, we can blow you away right here and shove you the rest of the way."

The gravel led to a cliff. It hung over a huge body of water that went on and on into the dark horizon. I didn't like my options at all. However, the first one would buy me a few more moments on Earth. I used my elbows, knees, and hands to get to my feet. My ankles remained fastened together as I bounced up and down. I moved at a slower pace, but I kept it moving.

"Make sure that gun stays on him!" the hype man bellowed.

Nighttime Shades frowned in his direction. "Man, I got this! You needs to chill with yo' tone, brotha'."

Hype Man stared him down. He hit him with a large amount of sarcasm. "Just don't let him get away, again. Luckily, he's tied up this time."

Shades kept the gun on me, but maintained eye contact with the hype man. They connected eyes like they either wanted to fuck each other, or fight each other.

After twenty or so more painful yards of hopping, we arrived at the edge of the cliff. The cold air forced the waves to crash into the rocks along the water below. I glanced over the horizon and could not locate the Sears Tower or *any* lights for that matter. Complete darkness lay before me. I had no clue of my location.

"You've reached the end of the line, partna'." The hype man stood back a few feet and gave his command. "Put his ass to sleep!"

Nighttime Shades aimed the gun at me.

I closed my eyes, and every muscle in my body tensed up. My

eyebrows came together. I desperately called for God in my mind. *It can't end like this!* I froze for several seconds and nothing happened. One eye crept open, and I took a peep at Nighttime Shades.

The weapon pointed at me, but he hesitated with the trigger.

"Lay his ass to rest, soldier!" The hype man got loud on him. "Shoot him!"

"Ask me nicely." Nighttime Shades came out of left field with his attitude. "I don't know who the hell you think you are, but it stops tonight. Right now, right here. Ask me nicely."

"What?" The hype man gazed at him like he was crazy. "You pick right now to try and flex? You tryna be a big man?"

"Just show me some respect, Paul. We about to hit this road, and you ain't gone be ordering me around like I'm a slave." Nighttime Shades kept me covered with the gun. "I'm not gone say it again. Ask me nicely, or you can lullaby this nigga yourself."

"See, that's what I'm talkin' 'bout right there. This is too much confusion." Hype Man's head tilted back and to the side. A smug expression accompanied his smirk. "The plan. Do it now."

Black and Silver reached under his coat and pulled a Glock from the rim of his pants. He popped a bullet in the hole and pointed it at the back of Nighttime Shade's head.

POW!

I jumped out my skin, but managed to keep my balance.

The bullet entered and exited his skull. Brains, blood, and bones exploded out of his forehead. The pistol fell from his hand. His body crumbled forward to the gravel.

What the hell, man? The turn of events threw me for a loop. *He just shot his own boy?*

"Good job." The hype man scurried to Nighttime Shade's corpse. "Now, help me toss his ass off the edge."

Black and Silver joined him in rolling the body to the brim of the cliff. They used their feet to kick Shades over the steep rock.

His body tumbled and rolled off the ledge. A few seconds of silence was eclipsed by a huge splash in the distance.

I cringed at witnessing another death and got sick at the thought that mine was coming next.

"Okay, let's drop this fool." The hype man gave his command to his sidekick as he led him toward me. "Put this clown's lights out."

Black and Silver stepped to me with his gun out. He pointed it directly at my face.

"Wait!" I panicked and tried to stall them. "Don't shoot! I ain't see nothin', man. I won't say a thing!"

The young kid popped a bullet in the hole.

CLICK!

"Don't do this, lil' homie." I lowered my tone to try and connect with him. "He's just gonna kill *you* next."

The youngster paused, blinked a few times, and soaked it in for a second.

It's gettin' to him! I got excited with the slim chance of establishing rapport. "Don't make the same mistake your boy made. C'mon, kid. Think about it."

"Naw, man. You're crazy. Paul wouldn't play me like that." He kept the gun on me as he spun his head toward the hype man. "Ain't that right, man. You wouldn't kill—"

POW!

The hype man pulled his trigger.

The bullet blasted through Black and Silver's head. His brains sprayed all over my face.

I ducked in reaction to the sound of the gun and in reaction to the insides of a human's cranium splattering against my mug.

Black and Silver's gun went off.

POW!

The bullet launched and propelled to the sky. The youngster's body stumbled my way and plowed into me.

We both crashed to the ground, and he landed on top. He crushed me as more of his opened crown spilled on my coat. The gun rolled off his fingers. I shoved him off and scooted across the ground in the opposite direction. *What have I gotten myself into?*

The hype man dragged Black and Silver's dead body to the edge of the cliff. I wrestled myself to my feet as he got rid of another corpse. *How high is this ledge?* I decided to count how long it took before the body hit the water. The hype man nudged him over. *One thousand one. One thousand two. One thousand three. One thousand four. One thou— Splash!*

Oh my God! Nerves shot through me from head to toe. *I'm next.*

Hype Man marched in my direction with his gun at his side.

Stall him! Talk him out of this! My mind raced out of control. "C'mon, Paul. Why you doin' this, brotha'?"

"It's for the money, dude. Them niggas was just dead weight." Each stride covered a lot of ground. He stopped a few yards in front of me. "The black market will pay millions to get their hands on the technology in these pills. I'm dumpin' this van and layin' low. Got enough dough from these last two hits to sneak my way into Mexico. Then the pills go to the highest bidder. And I'm set. That music shit wasn't gonna pay off. MC ET would've never gotten a record deal."

"You still don't have to do this, dog." I hit him with desperate pleas. "Just let *me* go. All is well with your plan, fam'. They ain't gone catch you either way it goes."

"Well, maybe. And maybe not." He popped a bullet into the hole and pointed the weapon at my forehead. "The bottom line is you've seen too much, and I can't take that chance. So say good night to the bad guy."

"Not so fast, Paul!" Kyle's voice came out of nowhere. "Drop the weapon, or I'll drop you!"

Chapter Twenty-two:
Ichabod Crane

What? I looked up and spotted my boy marching toward us like the cavalry. Kyle pointed his shotgun at the hype man.

"Set it on the ground nice and slow, playa'. Then take a couple steps backward," he said.

Hype Man rushed me and snatched me up by my elbow. He gripped me tight as hell as he shoved the barrel of the Glock under my chin. "Think twice about what you do next, old man."

Kyle took consistent steps to his right. He squinted one eye as he sized up his target. "Don't make me blow you away, lil' brotha'."

"I know you ain't gone do nothin' foolish. Are you?" The hype man twisted me around as he moved to keep Kyle in perfect view. You don't want your boy's face to get blown off, do you?"

"Naw, we don't want that." Kyle kept the barrel on him. "And we don't want you to catch this round in your chest, either. Do we?"

"Go ahead, Kyle!" I yelled my approval to pull the trigger. "Blow his fuckin' head off!"

"Shut up!" The hype man mashed the pistol in my chin even deeper.

It choked me a little. *Mutha*— I wanted to elbow the hype man in his gut, and then dive to the side, so Kyle could blow his dome full of pellets.

"Now, we have two choices. We can handle this like gentlemen," Kyle said as he moved closer to the edge of the cliff. He kept his eye on his target. "Or, we can get into some gangsta' shit."

No he did not come with the Max Julien line from The Mack. I may have laughed if it were not for the gun at my head.

"Oh, you gone quote Snoop Dog on me, huh?" The hype man was serious. He tightened his grip on my arm. "You ain't think I knew about that, old man. Did you?"

What? This clown was definitely born in the nineties. I really wanted Kyle to shoot his young ass at that point.

"Yeah, right. Snoop Dog." Kyle reached the ledge and rested only twenty-five yards away from us. He stepped in our direction.

"Come any closer, and he dies!" The hype man repositioned the gun to emphasize he meant business. It pointed at my Adam's apple. "Don't test me!"

Kyle froze in his tracks. He stood well within shooting range. The shotgun barrel aimed in our direction. "Give it up, Paul. This is your last chance."

"Fuck you, and fuck him! I bet I can shoot both of y'all before you could hit me once from there with that thing." Hype Man moved the pistol from my throat to between my eyes. "You niggas don't stand a chance against me!"

Kyle went silent. He placed all his concentration on his aim.

Wow, he's gonna shoot for real! I debated on my next move. *Should I stand here or dive away?*

The hype man didn't wait to see what Kyle planned to do. He pulled the gun from my face and pointed the barrel in Kyle's direction.

WHAM!

An aluminum baseball bat whirled into the scene. It walloped the hype man between the shoulders in the back of his neck.

"Ah!" Hype Man griped in distress. His arms flew into the air, and he dropped to the ground face first. The gun rolled off his hand. He rested there, motionless.

My eyes bucked. *What the hell just happened?* I glanced around at my nephew standing over the hype man like he was ready to take another swing if necessary.

Astonished, I called his name. "Dorian?"

"It's me in the flesh, Uncle Dre." He used his foot to shove the gun away from the hype man.

Kyle lowered his weapon and jogged to our side.

"But what're you doing here?" I asked in confusion. "How'd you—"

"He hid in the back of your truck." Kyle rested the end of his gun on his thigh and pointed the barrel to the sky. "After they caught you and put you in their van, I jetted back to your ride. Luckily, I found your nephew, and he had an extra set of keys. So we followed y'all here, snuck up, parked on the other side of that field house, and came up with a quick plan."

And it was well executed. I specifically told Dorian he couldn't roll with me. However, I'd never been so happy to have a rule broken in my entire life. *He's growing up.*

Dorian poked at the hype man with the bat. He didn't budge. Kyle scooted the hype man's gun away with a stick. He nudged the other handguns into a pile several yards away.

I made eye contact with my nephew. "I told you to stay at the crib. You know you are *so* grounded."

We cracked up. Kyle returned and slapped Dorian on the back. They stood over the hype man's motionless body.

I hopped toward them and collapsed to the ground. Everything ached and throbbed from head to toe. "I know y'all feeling like Alex Cross and Virgil Tibbs right about now. Ya' know? Big time black detectives and what not. But can somebody help me outta these cuffs? It's some tools in that van."

Dorian jogged away to find something to use to clip the binders.

"That kid is just about all grown up," Kyle said.

"Yeah, it won't be too long before he's out and on his own," I replied. *It seems like my sister just gave birth to him yesterday.* The few clouds in the sky cleared and allowed the stars room to sparkle. "Where are we anyway? This don't look like no Lake Michigan to me."

"It's not," Kyle replied. "We're just across the border in Indiana. This is Wolf Lake. I-90 is right outside this park."

Dorian trotted back with his bat in one hand and a pair of shears in the other. He squatted and clipped the plastic around my ankles.

SNIP.

I spread my legs apart. *What a relief.* It felt like I'd just got off a plane, or I'd just taken off some roller skates or something. I sat up. "Now get these things off my wrists."

Dorian came at me with the shears.

"Hold it." Kyle grabbed Dorian's arm. "Wait a minute. I kinda like him like this. You have any demands you wanna make before we release him?"

My nephew chuckled. "Ummm. I don't think so."

"Oh, no. You gotta take advantage of your uncle and get something outta this. He didn't even want you to come, and you just saved his life." Kyle slapped Dorian on the back. "Come here. Lemme school you on how to milk a parent."

Dorian followed Kyle as they strolled away toward the field house.

I played along with them. "Hey, y'all gone just leave me right here?"

"We're gonna grab the truck and come around to scoop you,"

Kyle yelled in my direction as they strolled on. "Meanwhile, Dorian's gonna figure out what he wants out this deal."

The gravel pressed against my ass as I sat there. The ground grew too cold, so I shoved against it and came to my feet. *What a night. We caught MC ET's killer.* I glanced at the hype man's body. *Where'd he go?* He no longer occupied the same space. Unbelievably, he'd vanished. *What the hell?*

SLAM!

The door to the white van shut tight.

"No!" I yelled to the top of my lungs.

Kyle and Dorian froze in their tracks.

You ain't goin' nowhere! I sprinted after the van in spite of my hands still being tied.

The engine started.

VROOM!

I scampered closer to the vehicle. With both feet planted on the ground, I leaped head first into the stratosphere. My arms shot out in front of me, and I sailed through the back doors. The interior slammed against my rib cage.

SCREECH!

Hype Man zipped out the parking space.

Momentum from him burning rubber pulled me toward the door. My feet slid out, followed by my legs and thighs. I snatched at the end of the bench. Both hands gripped it as my arms extended and my elbows locked.

The driver opened up the engine and put the pedal to the metal. Both doors flopped back and forward as I dangled outside them from the chest down. The duffle bags bounced around the van. One of them tumbled over my body, out the door, and dropped to the concrete. I gripped the bench with all my might. The ground rocketed past behind us. The duffle bag and the field house got smaller and smaller as we whizzed off.

Dorian and Kyle ran at us, but we left them in the dust.

The hype man raced away at top speed. A knee came up, and I got a toe into the interior. My fingers slipped a little, but I pulled the other leg up and climbed away. Both feet met at the heel of the door, and I vaulted myself the rest of the way inside. I used my elbows to push myself up to a squatting stand on my toes like Spider Man. The bench helped me keep my balance as I advanced on the killer.

Our eyes connected in the rearview mirror.

He slammed on the brakes.

SCREECH!

I stumbled forward. The force pulled me off my feet and flipped me into a somersault. I sailed through the air in a ball, head to the floor, crashing back first into the passenger seat.

BAM!

"Oh!" The day's pain intensified with the whack to my upper body. I slithered to the turf. My head hit first and my body tumbled over.

Hype Man put the van in park. He climbed over the gearshift and pounced on me. His fist stroked a right cross to my chin.

WHAP!

My face snapped to the side. Blood oozed across my taste buds as I pulled my knees to my torso. I planted my feet in his chest and drove his body into the ceiling.

He flopped to the floor and groaned in agony for a split second. I rolled to a sitting position and noticed him grabbing onto the plasticuffs. He slid his body out the van and landed on both feet as he bent his knees. Using both hands, he yanked the cuffs and dragged me along the floor on my stomach.

I sailed out the van and plummeted to the pavement chest first.

The hype man wound up his leg and kicked me in the upper body.

"Ow!" I curled up in a ball. *No more pain! I've had enough!*

He climbed into the van, stumbled through the interior, and

sat in the driver's seat.

I saw stars and wanted to give up. But I lifted my head from the pavement. *I told you that you ain't goin' nowhere!*

The van jerked as he slammed it into gear. I thrust myself to a standing position and leaped onto the bumper. My hands snagged the roof of the van.

SCREECH!

The hype man bolted off in the ride as I did a balancing act and clung on with all my might. The cold air smacked me in the face. My wrists remained fastened together. I glanced over my shoulder and caught Kyle and Dorian tailing in the Blazer at speeds way over the limit.

I ducked my head and climbed inside. The bench again worked as a balancing beam.

The van hit a huge bump and sprung into the air. I flew off my feet and slammed against the ceiling. The ride slam-dunked me to the floor face first. The hype man struggled to regain control of the wheel as we bumped and bounced around. One of the remaining duffle bags rammed me in the side of the head.

I landed beside the bench and gazed inside the storage area beneath it. *There's my shotgun!* My wheels turned on how I could shoot the rifle with the plasticuffs on. I rolled over on my back with my feet toward the driver and grabbed the weapon. Both hands slipped underneath next to the trigger. I let the butt of the gun rest on my stomach. The inner arch of my foot guided the barrel. Visually locked in on the back of the driver's head, I kept the muzzle still with my shoe and peeped through the sight.

"Good night, bad guy." I pulled the trigger.

POW!

Pellets shot from the gun and drilled their way inside the hype man's cranium. His head flung forward, and the van veered to the left.

Propulsion tossed me in the opposite direction. I rolled over and slammed into the bench.

WHAM!

The van zigzagged to the right. I tumbled around until I crashed into the opposite wall.

BAM!

I got dizzy, but managed to pull myself to a position where I could sit up.

The hype man lay sprawled out across the steering wheel. Blood gushed from his head as the van rolled along at top speed. The edge of the cliff approached outside the windshield. The van bounced around as it zoomed toward the ledge.

Oh shit! The shotgun fell, and I sprung over to all fours. I dragged myself up, hunched over, and sprinted toward the rear of the ride. The land outside the back door pulled away from me as the van neared the cliff. The front wheels dipped off the side of the mountain and the bottom of the car gave out.

I planted both feet on the rear bumper and launched myself into the sky. My hands shot out in front of me as I sailed through the air.

The back wheels rolled off the cliff. The van propelled over the peak and nosedived in the direction of the rocks and water below.

I flew through the heavens until I crashed chest first against the ledge.

WHAM!

My arms extended and wrapped over a small tree stump. I curled around it and held on tight, desperately kicking and kicking at air. I stretched my legs to find something I could secure a foot on, but felt nothing as gravity tugged and yanked at my feet.

Don't look down. I failed to listen to myself and glanced over my shoulder.

The van descended to the Earth and rammed head-on into the rocks beside the lake.

CRASH!

I dangled from the cliff, breathing at a rapid pace. *Now come on, man. Don't panic! Hang on! Don't fall! Don't let go!*

KABOOM!

The vehicle exploded. An orange ball of flames shot up from the wreckage and rose toward me. It morphed into black smoke.

I gripped onto the tree stump for dear life. My muscles shook and shivered like crazy. I swung hundreds of feet above the raging fire, suspended in midair. *Help!* I wanted to scream, but feared the energy it took to talk would lessen my chances to keep a grip on the tree.

"Hang on, Uncle Dre!" My nephew's voice approached.

"Don't let go!" Kyle's voice came next. "We got you, fam'!"

My partners rushed to me as they both hooked an elbow into mine. They tugged away, and I slid up the side of the cliff. I got far enough to help myself over the hump with my feet. The three of us scooted away from the ledge. I stopped to rest with them on either side of me. Black smoke from the fire rose to the sky before our eyes.

I chilled on my ass as I huffed and puffed away. "Man, y'all fools saved my life again. Thanks."

"You're welcome," Kyle replied as he caught his breath. "Just be warned, though. Twice a day to save someone's life is my limit. If you get into any more trouble over the next twenty-four hours, you're on your own."

We smirked and chuckled at the unbelievable experience we shared.

"One of those bags fell from the van." Dorian sprung to his feet and ran to the truck. "We scooped it up as we chased behind you. I wonder what's in it."

He returned with the black duffle bag and the shears. Dorian dropped the blades and unzipped the duffle bag in front of us. Several smaller plastic bags twist-tied shut were full of red pills.

"What's that?" My nephew's curiosity popped off. "Ecstasy?"

I stared into the sack in disbelief. "No, it's a different kind of drug."

"What we gone do with it?" Dorian asked. "Keep it?"

I concentrated for a few seconds to figure out the best move. *What would Doug do?* "You both have cell phones. Right?"

"Yeah, I got mine?" Kyle pulled his out his coat.

"Got mine, too." Dorian held up a phone with a blank screen. "But I turned it off when I hopped in the back of the Blazer. I didn't want it to vibrate, light up, or do anything."

"Hold up." *This has to work to our advantage somehow.* My wheels turned and turned as I glanced at my nephew. "Okay, check this out. Dorian, don't turn your phone on 'til you get home."

"Okay," he said. "But why not?"

"Nobody knows you're here. And from what Doug says, they can't retrace your phone if it's not on." I used my elbows to help me stand. "Somebody cut me out these cuffs."

"So we're not turning the bag over to the cops?" Kyle wanted to know my thought process as he snipped the plasticuffs off me.

"No, we're gonna drop Dorian off with it near the expressway," I advised as I waved my arms free, "and put him in a cab."

We scrambled to the truck and zipped away from the forest preserve. Luckily, we spotted a cab within three minutes.

"Take this bag home and hide it." I made sure I gave Dorian clear instructions. "Don't turn on your phone until you get there. You were never here."

The cab took off with my nephew and the black duffle bag. Kyle and I scooted around to the scene of the fire like we never left. We wiped down the bat and the shears and tossed them in the back of the truck. Next, we got our story together so as not to make a mistake when it came to Dorian's presence or the duffle bag. After that, Kyle called five-O.

I let the front seat back as we faced the lake. Smoke cascaded to the sky as the sun came up over the horizon. The lake extended for miles. A thick forest surrounded it on all other sides. *What a view.* Every bone and muscle in my body throbbed as police sirens approached in the distance. Exhaustion kicked in like crazy. I couldn't keep my eyes open another second as I dozed off.

Chapter Twenty-three:
A Month Later . . .

Man, I flew in the air about five thousand feet." I got loud as I exaggerated my tale. "Right through the clouds next to a 747 and shit. The pilot looked out the window at me all funny like he was shocked. Then he waved at me."

"Every time you tell that story it gets wilder." Doug sat across from me with a beer in his good hand. A sling held his other arm close to his body. "And you've got my king on the run. The pilot waved at you, huh?"

"Yeah. Then I glided down and landed on both feet like a pimp. The van crashed and blew up like a nuclear bomb." I moved a rook forward and captured one of his pawns. "Mate in three."

"What a story, though." Doug set his bottle on the table and moved his queen two spaces to the right. "You ever going back to work?"

"Ha, ha. Very funny, muthafucka." The job suspended me thirty days for having a positive drug test. I slid a rook forward and glanced at my watch. "Actually, it's gonna be cool to get back out there. I'm lookin' forward to it. Check."

"Good, 'cause I'm starting to get tired of you coming over here all the time." Doug already knew I'd be returning to work in two days. He appreciated me falling through during his recovery. But he thought I took the time off to deal with stress. He moved his knight forward. "Let's see if you can you deal with that."

"Nice move. But I've been keeping sharp all these years while you've been chasing bad guys." I moved a pawn forward one space. "Check."

"Wow, I'm in a tight spot. I've only got one move." Doug glanced across the board and blocked the path to his king with a bishop.

"Checkmate. And that's a good thing, 'cause I need to get outta here, man," I said as I rose to my feet. "What's this surprise you wanted me to see so badly?"

"It's actually two things. Hang on, bro. It won't be too much longer." Doug got up from the table and peeped through the blinds in his living room window. "As a matter of fact, here's part one now."

Ding-dong. The doorbell sounded off. Doug hurried to open it.

A tall, blonde, *America's Next Top Model* looking woman strolled in like she'd been there before. Doug greeted her with a peck on the lips as he took her coat. They marched over and stood before me with smiles plastered on their faces like The Joker.

"Andre, this is Brittany." He introduced me to his guest.

She extended her hand to shake mine. The lady posed in blue jeans and an orange sweater.

A white girl? I caught myself from saying the first politically incorrect thing that came to mind. Upon staring at her, I discovered another surprise. *It's the nurse from the hospital. Look at Doug.* I gazed at her in amazement.

Her hand dangled in front of me *as she smiled. "Doug said you would be caught off guard."*

Awkward. Once I realized I'd left her hanging, I shook her hand. "Oh! My bad, I'm sorry."

"This is my new friend." Doug confirmed he hit it already by saying that. "We met at the hospital."

As far as I recalled, Doug was the white guy that always liked black girls. On that tip, he reminded me of Robin Thicke or Roger Ebert or somebody. Seeing him with a white girl threw me for a loop.

"Dre, snap out of it." Doug snapped his finger in front of my face a few times.

"Wow, I apologize, again." I blinked twice and smiled. "It's nice to meet you."

"I wanted to surprise you, and it looks like it worked." Doug paused. "You can stop shaking her hand now."

"Oh, this is embarrassing as I don't know what." I released her hand and raised both eyebrows.

She laughed out loud. "It's okay. Doug's getting a kick out of introducing me to you like this. He knew you'd be unprepared."

"I know you're pressed for time," he said, "so I'll show you what's next on your way out."

Doug lived in a small ranch-style home, perfect for one person. Two bedrooms and an attached garage completed the layout. He led the way to the back. Brittany and I followed. He opened the door to the garage and flipped on the light switch.

"This is it." Doug leaned on a dark gray 2006 Toyota Corolla with tinted rear windows. "It's the new ghetto Batmobile."

"Oh, snap! That's what's up." I showed some excitement about his replacement work ride. "This car ain't as old as the other one. But does it have heat in the trunk this time?"

"Yep. Plus, it should blend in even better just about anywhere. That's the main thing. Can't wait for you to see it in action." Doug displayed a sense of pride. "Detective Timms tossed a job my way, and I'm gonna take it."

"You goin' back out there already?" I thought he should take some more time off. "Your shoulder okay enough to be tryna take a bite out of crime?"

"This ain't nothing but some surveillance. No big deal," he said.

"All right, man. Be careful out there, playa'." I slapped him five. "Ya' boy gotta get outta here. The clock is tickin'. Call me later on my cell."

Doug widened his eyes in surprise. "You gotta new phone?"

"Yeah, a smartphone. I never found my old one. It's time to get into something new anyway." I pulled out a brand new advanced device. "Now all I need to do is learn how to use it."

"Get your nephew to help you," he said.

"That sounds like a plan." I thought about Dorian and remembered I had news to share. "Oh, yeah. I meant to tell you. He's decided to go away to Northern and major in criminal justice. Just like his uncle."

"That's good, man. Tell 'im I said congratulations. I know you gotta get outta here, man. Good luck," he said. "Break a leg!"

The Blazer started up and I hit the expressway. The sun shined brightly, and the temperature made it up to forty-six degrees. The announcer's voice flowed out the radio. *"This is DJ Special Blend from Chicago. Only fourteen murders in the city for the month of February. That's fourteen too many. But at the same time, that's thirty-nine less than last month. Let's keep that trend going in the right direction, Chicago! Get 'em!"*

Hundreds of people lined up outside the House of Blues as I rolled up Dearborn Street. The line stretched across the bridge hovering over the Chicago River, and went all the way to Upper Wacker Drive. I pulled into the parking lot and flashed my concert badge to the valet. Several people with cell phones recorded me strolling into the building. I signed four autographs and posed for a picture with a young lady in the lobby. One of the ushers pointed me to the dressing room.

"We wondered if you were gonna make it." Kyle greeted me as I strolled in.

"Had a quick stop to make, but it's on like a pot of neck bones." The door shut behind me as I hung my coat on a hook. "We're doin' The House of Blues, and it's packed outside in case y'all ain't know."

"We got lucky to hook this gig up. But don't get it twisted." Logic dropped from Kyle's mouth. "Those people aren't here to see us. We're just the opening act."

"I don't know about that." Greg checked in with his opinion. He kicked back on a couch against the wall. "I heard the show wasn't sold out until they announced *us* on the bill."

"Be that as it may, we gotta keep our heads on straight." Kyle took charge of the moment. He went to his bag and handed envelopes to Greg and me. "Been waiting for the right time to give this to you cats."

Greg's face showed just as much confusion as mine. I ripped open the plain white envelope and slid out a check. *Sixteen hundred thirty-seven dollars and sixty-one cents.* Greg and I held our checks up so the other could see. The amount matched on each.

"What's this?" I asked.

"Royalties on sales." Kyle stood tall with his chest out. "I uploaded "Hip-Hop Villains" for sale to the Internet. So we picked up some loose change. And that's just the beginning. Got another check for y'all coming soon from ASCAP."

Wow. I was happy to see the check. However, my conscience ate away at me. And this brought on the opportunity to do something about it. Not a lot, but something. "I'm giving this money to Simone's family, along with any more checks I get from that song. Forever."

"What?" Kyle jerked his head back and raised one eyebrow. "Are you sure about that? Forever is a mighty long time."

"I'm positive." I couldn't put a dollar sign on that young man's life. But I felt like I owed them big time. "His family can have it all."

"Man, that's a nice gesture." Greg gave his approval as he came to his feet. "I'm giving my cut to the church. It's going straight to the building fund."

The three of us posed in silence. Greg and I glanced at each other, and then we both stared at Kyle.

"Y'all some good people." He raised his palms and dipped his shoulders to the side. "Way better than me, 'cause I'm keeping mine all to myself."

We chuckled and met in the middle of the dressing room.

"Naw, but for real. I'm glad to see us back together again." Kyle acted like he wanted to get all emotional.

"Well, you know. I think I can have a bigger influence on more people in the public eye like this." Greg stretched his arms as we prepared to go on stage. "Gotta spread the good word of the Lord."

"Well, spread some of the Lord's good word across us before we go on stage," I said.

Greg closed his eyes as he prayed, "Heavenly Father, watch over us as we take this stage . . ."

As with every show the three of us did together, Greg prayed us onto the stage. I welcomed this peaceful scene after all the violence and death I'd recently witnessed.

". . . in Jesus' name we pray, amen." Greg opened his eyes and gazed at us.

Our hands piled on each other. On three we said, "Inner City Youth!"

We took the stage. The crowd at the House of Blues went bananas. Thanks to the radio, they knew the words to both our songs and spit right along with us. Several times, Kyle persuaded the people in the audience to grab their phones and download our music. We rocked the stage and got all up close and personal with the crowd. They screamed our stage names like never before. It was exactly what we dreamed about as kids. Our set ended with "Hip-Hop Villains." We each rocked two verses, and I went last on that song.

During the final verse, a figure in the backstage area caught my attention out the corner of my eye. I glanced at the person several times and recognized the man as the janitor from the first concert. *Yeah, that's him!* Curiosity got the best of me, and I needed a close up view of this man's face. I wanted to know if he actually saw anything the night of the triple murder. *Heck, is that my old man? No, that's crazy.*

He smiled and made distant eye contact with me for a brief moment. The old man strolled away.

I wanted to drop the mic in the middle of my verse and run after him. But that would've been unprofessional. We dusted off our routine and bowed to the crowd, twice. I ran backstage and glanced around. The janitor was nowhere to be found. I dipped through the hallways outside the dressing rooms and searched all the way to the lobby area. The janitor disappeared.

Humph. That spooked me a little, but I didn't spend too much time on it. *Maybe I'm just missin' my old man a lot right now.* I let it roll off me and enjoyed the moment in time.

The press released the true identity of the murderer. Stallion Pee kicked it in jail for violating his parole. Add that to being a suspect in this case, and it boosted his record sales. Mix show DJs and radio stations pumped our music like crazy following the events. The papers and blogs went nuts about our story. Solving the mystery and finding the killer helped us get lucky and receive another fifteen minutes of fame. It felt good to perform again, but my attention soon focused on one last matter of business I needed to face.

The next day, I gave Antoinette Miller a call. We agreed to

meet in a public place. Once again, Evergreen Plaza served as the spot. The temperature got all the way up to fifty-seven degrees that Sunday afternoon in early March. I parked underground around the back as usual.

The black duffle bag hung over my shoulder as I stood in the middle of the center square. *It's hard to believe this place is about to close.* I scanned the upstairs and downstairs until I caught her silhouette coming around the corner. She stepped up and stopped a yard in front of me.

The sight of her made my skin crawl. I wanted to choke the hell out of her. Steam came out my ears, but I kept my composure.

We stood there in silence for a moment.

I took the initiative and spoke first. "I have something for you."

Chapter Twenty-four:
The Meeting

Thanks for finally calling me back and meeting with me." She spoke with a soft and humble voice. "I just want to say thank you."

"Really now?" I raised one eyebrow and stared her down. "What exactly are you thanking me for?"

"Finding my son's killer." She closed her light brown eyes for a tick as if to pray. "The police would've never caught them. You and Doug brought on justice."

She's so full of shit. I twisted my lips to the side. "Is that what this is really about? Straight up, Antoinette. Save that song and dance for Doug. I know the real deal."

"I tried calling you, Andre." Her eyebrows went up in the middle, and she busted out the famous cry face. "Why'd you block my number? I just wanted to say thanks."

"No, you wanted to know if you were gonna lose your job." It was hard to keep my voice at a respectable level. "You sent me and Doug out to risk our lives, and it was because you didn't want to lose your job. Say it."

"Oh, stop it." Guilt hit her for a half second. She snapped right out of it and an attitude took over. "I'm not gonna say anything. I'm not a child."

"You got a lotta nerve getting snappy with me. And it's real hard to keep my cool right now." I took a deep breath and glanced around at my surroundings. "I'm heated with you. You told me Eric was my son. How low of a person are you?"

Her eyes watered. She tightened her lips and looked away from me. "He *was* your son."

"He was, huh?" I took a step forward and frowned as hard as I could. "I brought this to Goldie's attention before he died. He told me it was bullshit. What's up with that?"

She froze as if she'd seen a ghost. Her mouth shot open wide, and she covered it with her palm. A tear ran down her cheek. She took a deep breath and lowered her head. "I'm sorry. At first, I knew I would have to tell you the truth one day. But I thought I could ride it out since Goldie passed away. Now, you tell me that you told him?"

"Yeah, I told him," I said, "and he said it was bullshit."

"Oh God, I wish that didn't happen. I found out I was pregnant after you got married. I knew it could possibly be yours or someone else's." She finally came forth with different information. Her eyes looked down, and her hands got all fidgety. "That somebody else was Goldie. We went to get a paternity test, and it proved Goldie was Eric's father. And he was a great father, indeed. Wow, I feel so bad he found out I dissed him by telling you that you were Eric's father. Now, I can't even tell Goldie I'm sorry."

"He ain't the only one you dissed. I'm a married man, Antoinette." I made this point to her before, but I didn't think she got it. "You presented me with that junk, and I betrayed my wife. What's wrong with you?"

"Okay, you're right. Andre, I was desperate. I didn't want to lose my job or more importantly, go to jail." A waterfall shot down her face as she confessed the truth. "If those pills get into the wrong hands, I'm up shit's creek with no paddle. I was wrong for seducing you, but I needed you to stay on the case. I never meant to hurt your wife. Just don't tell her what happened between us."

"I did already." I folded my arms across my chest as I stood at attention. "Guilt ate at me too much, so I told her everything."

"Oh no, Andre! You shouldn't have done that." She looked at me like I was crazy. "What happened when you told her?"

"Well, that's none of your business. That's up to my wife and me to work out." The duffle bag dropped off my shoulder and hit the floor. I shoved it in her direction with my foot. "Here. I told you I had something for you. This is what you disrupted my life for. Your motivation is right here in the bag, sweetheart."

She frowned up in confusion, and then shot to her knees. Antoinette fumbled around with the sack like a kid opening up a present on Christmas morning. She glanced inside. "Oh my God! This is it!"

"Yeah, that's it. That's what you've been wanting back. You couldn't ask the cops if they saw it. Neither could you ask Doug. I know you've been burning up inside to know what happened to the stash. Well, there it is."

"Wow, I can't believe it. It looks like it's all here." All of a sudden, Antoinette realized she was in the middle of a mall and shut the zipper tight on the bag. She returned to her feet. "I don't know what to say. Thank you!"

"Whatever. Take your fancy, top-secret drug. Just stay away from me and my family." I thought about it for a second and added another stipulation. "Oh yeah, stay away from Doug, too."

"Andre, you're still a good man. Thanks again from the bottom of my heart. You had every reason to turn me in, but you didn't. Maybe you're too angry with me to hear this right now, but I'm *mostly* upset about losing my only child. Really, thank you for finding my son's killer." She picked up the duffle bag and put it on her shoulder. "It's too bad you endured everything you went through. If it helps, please let your wife know that I'm sorry."

"Why don't you let her know yourself," I said.

"Yeah, tell me yourself." Colisa's voice rang down out of nowhere.

Antoinette's eyes grew large. She whirled around.

My wife settled before her with a frown on her face.

"Oh my God!" Antoinette froze in her tracks. Her mouth opened wide as all outside. "Wow, I don't know what to say."

"Well, I know exactly what to say. And I'm only gonna say it once. Bitch, stay the *hell* away from my husband!" Colisa pulled back her elbow. She shattered her fist into Antoinette's chin.

WHAM!

INNER
CITY
YOUTH

About the Author

Robert Fain DJ's and writes under the name
DJ Special Blend from Chicago. He can be heard
faithfully hosting Chicago's longest running
Hip-Hop podcast at **BMSRadioChicago.com** and
can be seen DJing private parties & corporate events
regularly throughout the Midwest. Rob likes his **Harold's Chicken**
fried hard with mild sauce, salt and pepper, with an extra cold slaw.
His favorite view of the sky line is from **31st Street Beach**. He cried
when **Walter** died and when **Benji** died, and he drove past
Comisky Park (US Cellular Field) seven times the night the
White Sox won the **World Series**.

Other titles from this author:
"The Benjamins"
"Witness to a Murder: The DJ Saw It"
"Witness to a Murder 2: In Too Deep"
"Witness to a Murder 3: House Music Picnic"

CITIFIED
PUBLICATIONS

http://www.CitifiedPublications.org
http://www.BMSRadioChicago.com

www.ingramcontent.com/pod-product-compliance
Lightning Source LLC
Chambersburg PA
CBHW050927120626
46552CB00001B/77